THE
WINE
CLUB
AN EROTICOGRAPHY

EDGE STEELE

Cover design, interior book design, and eBook design
by Blue Harvest Creative
www.blueharvestcreative.com

Published by
Zinful Press

ISBN-13: 978-0692215791
ISBN-10: 0692215794

Visit the author at:
www.facebook.com/edge.steele
www.twitter.com/EdgeSteele
www.edgesteele.tumblr.com

THE
WINE
CLUB

ONE

IT WASN'T ALWAYS THIS WAY

Things were different before I met her. I was working a security gig, checking badges, pretending to greet people with a smile, degrading stuff really after where I had been, employed as a cop at night in the worst area of the most dangerous city in the state. Making a difference and battling night after night with drug dealers, gang bangers, and watching my back, as my fellow cops were not much better than the people I arrested. The constant stress had taken its toll and I had to take a different, less stressful job.

The days of monotonous standing, greeting people, checking government badges, and allowing them access to the facility had lulled me into a softened state. I was no longer as edgy or alert and started to entertain myself, checking out the occasional attractive woman who came through the gate. One in particular got my attention. She was an administrator, an officer actually, but from my viewpoint not like the rest. Several female officers came through. Most were unattractive, butch as hell and arrogant bitches. I would have found a way to write them a ticket a few months earlier. In this job, I had to eat my pride, smiling and replying, "yes, ma'am" to their conceited demands. The officer whose credentials I now checked was as self-centered as the rest, but on her first trip through the gate, I noticed as I looked down at her sitting in the vehicle, she wore the typical military office worker's skirt.

What made her different was that she wore thigh high nylon stockings. As she sat waiting impatiently for me to allow her access, I just saw the elastic that held them up. I made a point out of making her wait a little longer than usual, staring at her long legs from behind my dark sunglasses. While the glasses protected my eyes from the bright sunlight glaring off the thousands of vehicles I checked daily, they also allowed me to visually check the insides of the vehicles without being noticed, looking for drugs, weapons and the rare flash of thigh high stockings. She came to the gate every day so maybe two or three days a week, I would catch a brief glimpse of the amazing pair of legs she kept barely hidden.

The months wore on and summer was in full-blown glory. The temperature had risen dramatically and I had traded the cold weather gear for short-sleeved shirts, although I kept the dark glasses. I guess I got too complacent because one day, while pretending to check the arrogant officer's badge, I was caught off guard. Usually on the street, nothing short of being shot at would faze me. Today it was exceptionally hot. The traffic was heavy as it was lunch hour and people were returning to work after a quick bite.

As the traffic poured in, I saw the officer with the thigh-highs one car back. I waited with anticipation as this was about the only positive aspect of this job. Rapidly checking the person in front, I waved her forward and watched as she approached, trying to get a glimpse of her thigh-highs. She caught me off guard, slowly pulling down the skirt she wore. Her legs were spread more than usual but enough for me to see that she wore no underwear. The thigh-highs were in place as usual and she cooled her smooth shaven pussy with the artificial breeze generated by the car's air conditioning. It was an amazing sight. I tried to catch as much detail of her swollen pink lips as I could without being obvious. I guess I was painfully obvious and a bit distracted.

She handed me her badge. I reached for it, but missed her hand and dropped the badge on the ground as I was watching her pull her skirt down to a more modest position. She became angry with me and I knew I was in trouble. For the first time, I had been caught looking up her skirt, gazing at her legs and beautiful pussy instead of doing my job. She glared at me and as I handed her badge back, she refused to move forward in the line of cars.

"What's your name, officer?" she said in a commanding tone.

I was instantly annoyed but had learned to play the game with these arrogant bitches.

"Officer Steele, ma'am, Edge Steele."

She rolled her eyes and said, "You've got to be kidding me. Who has a name like that?" Laughing in a condescending manner she added, "Well, Officer Steele, if you want to keep your job, you'd better find a way to be more professional than you've been today. Do I make myself clear?"

The bitch would never have talked to me this way on the street, never! However, I wasn't on the street. I needed this job to survive.

I paused then answered through clenched teeth, "Yes ma'am."

She rolled up her window and quickly departed the gate, watching me in her rear view mirror. I saw she was just as furious for her own reasons.

A few hours passed. I tried to forget the sight of her slightly spread legs, and the irritation I felt at being caught and spoken to like I had been a criminal for looking at her. What the hell did she expect? Was I really not supposed to look as she cooled off in such a provocative way? Fuck this! I wasn't a pervert. I was a normal guy.

I barely heard the phone ringing in the office we used to protect ourselves from the weather and to relax in during the rare breaks in traffic. Finally, I came out of my angry stupor and realized it had been ringing for some time. I stopped the traffic and entered the small building to answer the phone.

"Officer Steele, may I help you?" I barked into the phone, impatient at the interruption.

After a pause, I heard a female voice on the line.

"Officer Steele, I'd like to think that your actions today are an anomaly. It's not every day I feel so violated when I come to work. I'm struggling with an appropriate way to deal with your behavior."

It was that same long-legged officer that had belittled me earlier; she wasn't going to let this go. I couldn't believe it. I was instantly pissed off but said nothing, letting her comments hang in the air unanswered, although I couldn't deny I had heard them.

She said, "I've decided for the time being not to talk to your boss. I'm not sure that's the appropriate thing to do, but I wanted you to know there should be consequences for your actions today. Am I clear on that point?"

I wanted to scream into the phone, "*Fuck you bitch!*" but instead, I barely managed to spit out through clenched teeth, "Yes I understand."

She replied, *"And?"*

I paused, thinking, what the hell did she want me to say? I knew I had better answer her because my job hung in the balance. She had me in a vulnerable position. I tried to think what she wanted to hear. Working with these arrogant people had taught me they expected you to be humble in their presence, apologetic and groveling. I wanted to strangle this bitch now. She wanted me to say, "Thank you ma'am, sorry for looking at your spread legs as you pulled up in your car."

I barely managed a broken, "I am sorry ma'am, please don't call my boss."

I hated how far I had fallen in life, apologizing now and asking for pity. I heard the satisfaction in her voice with my response. She reminded me that she couldn't promise anything, that my behavior was alarming and she would need to consider it. Perhaps, she said, she would ask around to see if this were a habit of mine. The line went dead.

This incident was more serious in this world of paper pushers and office workers than it would be on the streets. As a cop, women throw themselves at you all the time. You get accustomed to the brazen flashing of tits and ass, and offers of casual sex. It is meaningless and if you want to stay a cop for more than a week or two, you learn to look and not touch. No harm, no foul. In this environment, however, I was already in over my head and the day was just halfway done.

Several days passed and I noticed the former panty-less officer coming through the gate, using other lanes than mine, but always watching me. I tried to pretend I wasn't aware of her, but I was. She held my immediate future in her hands. If she decided to contact my boss I would be unemployed a fleeting few minutes later. She said nothing, however, and her cold hard glare gave no hint of anything good coming out of this incident.

A couple of days later, I was leaving the gate for lunch. We were allowed a brief escape from the gate to go to a nearby restaurant and get a sandwich. I crossed traffic lanes walking to the white Chevy Tahoe we used to get food, and saw the same female officer watching me, two cars back. I tried not to feel anxious at her intense stare. I couldn't escape this bitch. I got in the Tahoe and left the area, heading to the sandwich shop. A few minutes later, I returned and sat down inside the concrete building to eat lunch. The phone rang again. There was a knot in my stomach. I never felt fear on the streets, but here I was out of my element, and in hers. I looked at the phone as it continued to ring. I didn't answer. I had quit chewing the sandwich and was deep in thought. What was I afraid of? She had not called my boss and we received calls on the phone frequently, so why was this phone call any different? I convinced myself I was being ridiculous and answered the phone. My heart pounded as she started to talk before I even finished my required official greeting.

"Officer Steele, do you go to lunch every day at this time?"

I didn't answer.

She said, "I asked you a question, I expect an answer, Officer Steele!"

I replied quietly, "Yes every day, I go to the sandwich shop to get lunch at about this time."

She replied, "Okay, well tomorrow at this time, I will expect you in my office, Building 1401. I'm the Executive Officer to General Rodriguez. You'll be able to find his office, it stands out. I expect you here at 11:30 sharp. Do I make myself clear?"

Ya, real fucking clear, I thought, but somehow I managed, "Yes ma'am."

Then I heard a voice that sounded far away asking her not to fire me, I needed this job, I had been a cop and had to leave the streets for personal reasons. This was the only job I could find. The voice sounded desperate and afraid, and I was surprised when I realized the voice was mine.

Following a pause, she replied, "That's not my concern, Officer Steele. 11:30 tomorrow sharp, it'd be wise not to be late."

The line went dead. I hung up, my appetite gone, and I threw away the sandwich.

The next twenty-four hours crept by slowly as I imagined the different scenarios that could play out. If the General himself called my boss to report what had happened, that wouldn't end well. Maybe I should just quit this damn job rather than be humiliated like this. That wasn't an option though, with bills, debt, and child support to pay. I would have to see this through to its end. I slept very little, but decided early in the morning not to show up to this meeting looking like shit. If I was going to be fired, I wouldn't look beat down. I felt beat down and afraid for the first time in years, but I didn't have to show it.

The hands on the clock ticked by slowly and at 11:20, I saw the bitch come through another lane. She made no eye contact with me at all. This wasn't good. I was going to be fired, that was a given outcome already but I decided no way was she going to get the best of me.

11:30, I walked to the Tahoe, got in and started the car, driving to the building she told me she worked in. I entered the air conditioned offices and looked at the directory near the door. The General's office was the third door down on the left and I walked to it, my heart pounding, dreading the outcome of this meeting. I opened the door and there, seated behind a massive desk, was the woman who had tormented me for the past three weeks. She was on the phone and from the conversation, I could tell that she was talking to someone she dated and they were discussing me. Shit!

She said, "Okay, he's here now, I have to go. I'll let you know how it goes. Love you too, bye."

I stood in front of her desk and she got up abruptly, walking around the large ornate desk. Her body language told me she was still upset: quick hand movements, flashing eyes, rigid thin lips. I was about to be fired, no doubt about it.

She marched right up to me, staring directly into my eyes, unflinching. I had to admit she was strikingly beautiful, and the presence she commanded in the office was intimidating and intoxicating at the same time. My mouth became dry and sticky as she started to explain what was going to happen today. I heard the words "terminated" and "unprofessional behavior that was unacceptable." All that mattered to me was that I didn't show her fear. I was afraid, I admit it. I had faced many dangers in the streets, but nothing made me shake like I did now.

Reality was, my whole life I had kept a terrible secret. Although I appeared to despise women and treated them like dirt, I wanted nothing more than to be the property, literally the property, of a strong, beautiful, and powerful woman. No man should feel this way, but I did. I was alone in this need, never having heard any other man mention feelings like this so I kept my secret buried and hidden.

Staring at her angry eyes and hearing my immediate future was un-employment, I couldn't help but smile. She was even more beautiful in my twisted mind here, in control, in her office, than she was that day legs spread in the car, cooling off and daring me to look. She stood inches from my face, talking quietly and powerfully. I noticed her eyes were even more intoxicating when she was in control, taking my life apart. I smiled again.

She replied, "Do you think this is funny, Officer Steele?"

I said quietly, "No, I do not."

"Why do you smile then? Don't you think I'm serious about this incident?"

Thinking about it, I had nothing to lose. I was going to lose my job, nothing would change that. While I thought, I heard a voice far away, confident and firm, saying her eyes were beautiful and that it was worth the loss of this shitty fucking job to see her legs spread apart.

"Ma'am, you are beautiful. I wouldn't change what I did that day for anything. I'll remember what you look like forever."

Silence between us. She stared at me, I stared back. Fuck it, I was going to be fired anyway, might as well spit out the truth.

She walked around her desk and pulled up the chair. Grabbing her mouse quickly, she started to work on some document. She hadn't told me to leave so I assumed I would be here until my boss met me and then fired me. I stood watching her. She banged lightly on the mouse. It wasn't working so she tapped it again. Nothing. Pushing the chair back, she looked into the darkness under the desk and cursed lightly under her breath. Abruptly, she stood up.

"Officer Steele, Edge Steele…what a ridiculous name! Anyway, would you look under my desk and reconnect my mouse? I kicked the cord when I got up to talk to you."

I thought about it. Actually, under any other circumstances, I wouldn't have considered it. The effect her presence had on me, our shared memory of her spread legs and swollen pussy that day made me want to stay in her office as long as possible. To help her in any way should have made me furious, but I was on autopilot. I wanted to tell her, "Hell no!" Instead, someone else made my feet move and I walked to her side of the desk. I got down and looked into the space in the desk made to accommodate her chair and legs. There was the disconnected cord, far back near the back of the desk. Her legs must be longer than I realized if she kicked that loose.

I said, "I do see the mouse cord."

"Could you connect it?"

"Yes, I'll have to crawl into the opening and reconnect it."

She said, "Do it then."

Just like that, no please, nothing grateful in that voice. Just a command, "Do it."

I got down on my hands and knees and crawled into the desk jockey's foot space. It was a humiliating moment to say the least and one of many to come. I heard her moving around behind me, then the sound of her chair rolling on the hard plastic that protected the carpet from wear and tear around the desk. Pushing the mouse cord into the computer, I turned around within the cavernous desk and was immediately wrapped up in a vice grip of legs and hands, forcing me angrily against that same swollen pussy I had caught a glimpse of before.

She whispered in an angry but sexy and desperate voice, "Is it as beautiful as you remember, you asshole? You have twenty-six minutes to make the most of this, Officer Edge Steele. Twenty-six minutes to save your fucking job. Eat my pussy like your job depends on it, bitch, because it does!"

She wasn't kind or gentle. With one hand firmly behind my head and the other holding the skirt she wore out of the way, she watched me while she rocked back and forth, rapidly grinding, pulling away briefly while I gasped for air. After she came violently, legs squeezing tightly against my head, her hand rigidly holding me in place ensuring I felt every spasm and tasted the cum as it flowed from her into my mouth, she lightened up.

Staring down at me, her legs spread wider, she said, "My, you're good at this. You have twenty more minutes, don't disappoint me, do you understand?"

I said, "I do."

This time, she was more relaxed and let me breathe when I needed to. She slid her chair deeper into the desk and started back to work. I was humiliated and elated at the same time. To be treated this way by anyone else would have been cause for a severe beating. I have to admit I fantasized about being owned like this, treated like property, like nothing more than a fuck toy. I'd never found a woman I would allow to treat me so poorly, and yet here I was with my lips willingly pressed against her, tongue exploring, tasting, and wanting this to never end. I heard myself moaning loudly.

She exclaimed, "You do like this, don't you?"

I hated to admit it, yes I most definitely did.

I felt her tense up and then heard a male voice in the room.

"So, what happened? Did you decide to fire the pervert?"

She stopped rocking her hips for a moment, unsure, I think, of what I would do.

She said, "No, he was so pitiful I felt sorry for him. So I told him to go back to his gate. I needed to think about it I guess. Do you think he should be fired?"

While I listened, I pushed her legs wider apart under the desk and started to really explore her pussy. Both her hands were above on the desk, and she couldn't stop me now without giving away where I was and what I was doing. I listened to them discuss my fate, her and her man, while I sucked hard on her clit and then flicked it repeatedly with my tongue.

I heard her comment about how warm it was in the room and that she felt flushed, then I felt her muscles tighten as she came again. She tried to fake a deep breath, as if trying to cool off because of the heat in the office. Her man misunderstood the comment she made and remarked about how he wanted to come to her place tonight and really heat her up with his cock. She agreed in a sexy voice that she couldn't wait and reached under the desk, telling her man she was wet just thinking about it and pretended to touch herself. Really though, she was caressing my head, and then she fingered herself while I licked her and stroked her thighs. They continued talking about their pending date later that night, and he told her how he really liked her appreciation of anal sex. He had never met a woman that enjoyed anal sex before and he liked that she experimented a lot sexually.

Pushing her legs further apart, I slipped my tongue as far into her ass as I could. She gasped. I heard her say, "I can almost feel your cock in my ass right now!" I slid my tongue back and forth from her ass to her clit, sucking and licking until he finally left.

She pushed her chair out of the hole in the desk, pulled her skirt down and said, "You can come out of there, now."

I crawled out of the desk, covered in her cum, my face slick and wet, smelling of her pussy, the taste of her ass still lingering on my tongue. I stood up and she faced me.

"I think I have a compromise, Officer Steele. This is not a choice. Do you understand me?"

I replied, "I do."

She said, "Until I tell you otherwise, you'll pleasure me on your lunch hour under my desk, just like you did today. I'll call you at your gate and you'll come here, get under my desk, and prove to me I haven't made a mistake in letting you keep your job. Do I make myself clear?"

She did, it was very clear that I had no choice, although I wasn't sure I wanted one.

She said, "From now on, you are my property. I want to hear you say it, that you're my property."

I couldn't believe the words slipped out of my mouth so quickly.

"I am your property," I heard myself saying in a voice that was deeply humiliated.

"Good! Now go back to work and Officer Steele, don't you dare wash your face until you get home or this deal is off. We clear?"

She was very clear.

As I left, she said, "By the way, my name is Athena, which is what you will call me from now on."

I went back to the gate deeply humiliated on one hand and on the other, feeling better than ever. So this is what it felt like to be a strong and powerful woman's property. I licked my lips as a test to see if the incident had really occurred. It seemed impossible the turn of events of the last half hour. The taste of her musky cum staining my lips and face told me it was, in fact, very real.

TWO

CHECK AND MATE

Another month passed and I started to wonder how long this mental mind game would continue. Somehow, I had been able to keep this on the down low, but people were beginning to notice my frequent trips to Athena's office. Reality was, this could only go on for so long and we'd get caught. I'd be fired for doing this, and she'd get me fired if I stopped or refused. We were in a mental chess match, and I was being outplayed at every move.

I stood at the gate again, checking identifications, watching people in cars as they rolled through. The repetition was mind numbing; eight thousand cars a day and all the attitude you could handle. Government employees are not happy, they are just employed. It was about 10:30. The sun was just starting to warm up and give a hint of the searing heat that would make the last part of the shift miserable. I reached out to collect the identification from the car that had just approached me and heard that familiar voice.

"Good morning, Officer Steele."

It was her again.

I was on auto pilot, tired and burned out from working two full time jobs to pay the bills and child support. Her sudden appearance startled me.

"Good morning ma'am, may I see your I.D?" I mumbled.

She ignored my comment and said, "I want you to come to my apartment tonight. I have some things to discuss with you. Be there at 18:30." She handed me a card with her address on it. "Make sure you're not late."

She started to pull away and I replied, "I can't make it. I have to work."

Stopping abruptly, she said, "Your shift ends at 15:00."

"Yes, for this job but I work two full time jobs. I leave this job and go immediately to another one and work until midnight."

She glared at me silently and then softened slightly.

"Is that why you're so tired all the time?"

"Yes, it is."

She said, "When is your next day off?"

I replied, "Friday, but I had planned to catch up on sleep."

She smiled and replied, "Well, your plans just changed! Friday then, 18:30 hours. *Don't* be late."

And she was gone.

The momentary loss of pain struck me again, and the way she so skillfully manipulated me. Ten minutes later, I realized I didn't even check her badge. Damn it! What the hell kind of hold did she have on me? What the hell was I going to do?

Anxiety rolled over me at the thought of being in her apartment. Hell, here I was at work in her office, under her desk performing like a trained pet and in a strange way, I looked forward to it. What would she do to me in the privacy of her apartment? I had no idea and could not imagine. The rest of the day was a mental battle, trying to plan a way out of this mess on one hand, painfully needing it and enjoying it on the other. I was a mess.

I didn't hear from her for the rest of the week. I looked for her at work, and one day caught a glimpse of her leaving the installation. She glanced at me momentarily as she passed in the outbound lanes. Her expression gave away nothing. Usually, I would have received a call telling me when to appear in her office for my daily humiliation, and lately I had to bring her a cold drink as well. These last few days, however, she hadn't called or come through my gate. The change had me on edge, curious, and strangely, I admit, I missed it.

Friday came and I was relieved to only have to work one job. I was happy to be free for a few hours from the daily grind of eighty plus hours a week. Finding the card she had given me, I looked up the address. The apartment was in a nearby city about half an hour from my condo. I left my place at about 6:00 p.m., thirty minutes before I was supposed to be at her apartment. I arrived on time, and as I got off the 1985 Honda Silver Wing CX-500 motorcycle I had ridden there, she pulled into the complex in her three-month-old fully loaded 2004 Honda Accord.

She pulled into a parking place and got out as the trunk lifted on the vehicle. Walking to the back of the vehicle, she removed a bucket filled with cleaning supplies: soap, window cleaner, chamois, paper towels, a bottle of Rain-X , a couple of cloths and a sponge. She walked up to me and handed me the bucket.

"You will wash my car while I work out at the apartment complex's gym." She walked past and pointed to the spigot on the side of the building. "You may get water there."

Then up the stairs she went to her apartment, never looking back. I sat there, stunned for a minute. Surprisingly, I did get water. I talked to myself under my breath, mumbling, "This is bullshit" every now and then as I started to wash the damn car.

I heard the door to her apartment open and she came down the stairs in brightly colored workout shorts and a tight fitting cotton t-shirt. She adjusted the ear buds of her MP3 player as I stopped washing the car to watch her walking down the sidewalk to the small gym in the center of the apartment complex. I had never seen her in civilian clothing before and it struck me how incredibly physically powerful she was. I knew that she was strong from the way she rode me as her daily desk bitch. There wasn't much about it that was tender or soft. It was hard and physically intense. Seeing her walk away, I realized I had never seen another woman like her. I continued to wash the car, quiet now, wondering what the rest of the night would be like.

Thirty minutes later, I finished washing and drying the car. As I was cleaning the windows, she walked up and stopped.

She looked the car over and said to me, "Don't forget to clean the windows inside the car as well, and the mirrors."

No "thanks." No "good job." Nothing but "Do this and do that." I didn't respond to the direction, I just did it. This night would be over soon enough, I was sure. I just needed to get through this.

I finished with her car and I admit, I did a good job. It wasn't really dirty to begin with, but now it shone! I collected up the supplies and turned towards the stairway to her apartment. The car chirped behind me and the trunk opened. She had been watching me from the balcony of her apartment.

She called down to me, "Put the bucket in the trunk and then come up, the door's open."

Doing as she said, I climbed the three flights of stairs to her apartment.

I opened the door and she called out, "Come in and sit at the counter. I'm nearly dressed."

She stepped into the hallway from the bathroom, nude, and watched to see if I looked. I didn't. The last time I snuck a peek up her dress as she came to work, I paid dearly. I wouldn't make that mistake again. She stood for several moments in the hallway, daring me to glance. I didn't, and finally I saw she was gone again in my peripheral vision.

I sat and waited at the small bar in the kitchen. She returned to the kitchen clothed, well sort of, if wearing a very sheer loosely fitting dress is clothed.

"Let's have some wine. Would you pick out a bottle from the fridge while I set the table?"

It was a question she had asked but the non-verbal communication was a statement, not a request.

I said, "I don't know anything about wine. I don't drink at all."

She stopped, turned, and looked at me.

"Are you serious?"

"Yes, I don't drink. I've been a cop for my entire adult life and I've seen what alcohol does to people's lives, so I don't drink. Ever."

She watched me carefully and said, "There's a bottle of Mirassou Pinot Noir in the fridge. It's quite good. Grab it and bring it to the table."

I got into the wine fridge, found the bottle and brought it to the table.

She said, "No, that's not a Pinot Noir, that's a Cabernet."

I replied again, "I don't know anything about wine."

Again the curious stare from her.

"Well, we'll have to change that," she said quietly, and I found the correct bottle in the small wine fridge. I returned to the table, and she opened then poured the wine into crystal glasses, spinning the wine in her glass and smelling the aroma.

Smiling, she held her glass to mine and said, "I have a toast."

I lifted the delicate glass in my hand, afraid I may break it.

She said, "To optimistic beginnings," and clinked the glasses together.

I didn't have a clue what the hell that meant, and she didn't elaborate. She was quiet and stared at me as I tried not to look at anything but her eyes. It wasn't easy to do. She was completely nude under the sheer dress. I wanted to look, I really did, but for some reason I couldn't. She continued to stare directly at me, comfortable, watching, and analyzing.

Finally she said, "I hope you like tuna steak. I prepared a nice one, and covered it with a sauce I made mixed with shitake mushrooms."

I hate tuna. I really hate tuna. I was going to have to gag this shit down or face her wrath. I didn't reply. I didn't want to lie or say, "I fucking hate tuna," either.

She finished with the food preparation and brought the tuna to the table. It was a huge steak of tuna. I looked at it wearily, covered with gravy and small bits of mushrooms. It was the biggest piece of tuna I had ever seen. Slowly picking up a fork, I broke off a small piece as she watched my every move. Her eyes were burning as I hesitantly raised the fork to my mouth for what will be the single most horrible meal I have ever eaten. My mouth exploded with flavors! I pushed back from the table and looked at her, startled.

She continued watching me and asked, "Is something wrong?"

There was a strange look on her face. I couldn't tell if she was angry, curious or just toying with me.

I blurted out, "Jesus, that is good! This is tuna?"

I cut off a bigger piece and shoveled it in this time with no hesitation.

She didn't reply for a few moments then commented, "You didn't like tuna before tasting this?"

I said, "No, I hate tuna. I mean, I really hate it, but this is amazing."

Another bite was already en route.

She didn't smile, or reply. She continued to eat her own meal and watched me.

"Try the wine with it, it pairs remarkably well."

I hesitated; I don't like wine, either. I lifted the glass, having not tasted it after the toast she had made and thinking back, I'd seen a look of disapproval on her face. She watched as I carefully sipped the wine. Again, my surprise must have been evident. It was amazing how well it complemented the tuna. I said nothing and took another sip, this one much larger. Warmth flowed down my throat, as I tasted a surprising mixture of spices, pepper, and fruit. She continued to observe, eating her own meal but taking note of everything I did and said.

I commented, "I am surprised the wine was so good. You're right about that as well!"

She ate in silence, and I was barely aware of her. The food was that good. When we finished, my mood improved dramatically.

She said, "Clean off the table and pour us more wine, then come sit on the couch."

I was up and halfway done with the task of removing plates and silverware, rinsing them in the sink before I realized I'd done it again! How did she do this? Here I was, doing these menial tasks without hesitation. I stopped and looked at her as she watched me intently from the couch. She noticed my puzzled look and I paused, feeling her eyes watching me again. For a moment, I had forgotten about her, forgotten that I was in her apartment and that she moved me around like piece on a chessboard.

I finished the plates and loaded the dishwasher, trying to regain some semblance of dignity. I took my time, trying to push back and make her wait for me to complete the task. Sitting on opposite ends of the couch, I faced straight ahead, feet flat on the floor. She sat comfortably on the opposite end, in a makeshift crossed leg fashion that kept her legs spread. The effect was excruciatingly painful. She was basically wide open; her body language dared me to look. Had I sat with any other woman posing like this, I would have taken it as a sexual offer. I didn't dare assume that in this context. Athena wasn't like other women. I stared straight ahead or down at my wine glass as she watched, amused at my obvious anxiety.

Finally she started to talk.

"Tell me what you're thinking."

I didn't answer.

"Edge! Look at me!"

I looked her directly in the eyes and she repeated, "Tell me what you're thinking and do not look away."

I stuttered and mumbled, but finally spit it out.

"I'm always confused about the way things feel when I'm around you. No man should feel like this! I'm on my knees under your desk whenever you tell me to be. I wash your fucking car without hesitation. I eat food that I know I'll hate and instead, find it's amazing. I shouldn't like how I feel and hate to admit it, but I do. I really do like how this feels. You're so fucking strong, and amazing and Jesus, the way you look! The way you taste! Did you know, I let you through the gate the other day and didn't even check your badge? What's wrong with me? No man should be so comfortable with this role. That's what I am thinking."

She said nothing for several moments, occasionally sipping her wine, never breaking eye contact. My frustration was obvious. The apartment was quiet except for discreet music playing in the background, of which I was just now aware. I recognized the group, "Lords of Acid," and the song was "I Sit on Acid." It was a dance song that played late at night on the radio on my way home from job number two. I commented on the song and that it fitted her. She smiled at that. I was getting angry at the frustration I felt, and started to push back again.

She said, "Tomorrow, you'll quit your second job. From now on, you'll be available to me after work whenever I require it."

"I can't quit the job, I need the money. I have child support and bills to pay. How will I pay that if I quit?" I asked.

"You will quit or I will have you fired from the job at the gate."

I was frustrated but nodded my head, saying nothing. I heard her voice, piercing my head like a lightning bolt.

"You don't realize it, but you're a rare find. You need to be owned. You're a submissive male and not just any submissive male. You don't even know it yet, that this is so rare. You fight it with every breath but it's deep within you. The need is instinctive in you. That's why you wash my car, clean the dinner plates. Honestly, try telling me you don't like being under my desk. Really, go ahead and try."

I heard a quiet voice, nearly a whisper.

"Yes I do."

It was my voice. I was barely aware of it, as I was lost in her piercing stare.

"Tomorrow, you will quit your second job. From now on, you belong to me. You'll be my property to do with as I please. There will be no argument. That job is over. About the money you need to pay bills, we'll talk about that later. From now on, you are mine."

I nodded in agreement. I had no choice anymore. A warm rush of adrenaline surged through me as I said nothing. I was painfully aware of an intense, barely contained need to be on my knees in front of her, serving her, pleasuring her, while she drank her wine. It was an extreme effort, but I didn't move. She smiled broadly, as if she could read my mind, and got up from the couch to pour more wine for both of us. Athena began to tell me about the wine, where it was made, and how. I listened intensely, absorbing everything I could. My education had begun.

A week later, she told me to arrive at her apartment. The change that had occurred was profound, and I was caught off guard as I realized it in a brief epiphany. She told me to choose a wine that would pair well with grilled steak. I picked a Malbec and opened it, pouring two glasses of wine.

She served dinner and asked, "How do you feel working only one job?"

I replied, "I feel much better, the exhaustion is fading. Thanks."

Wham! It hit me how comfortable I was serving her. Somehow she knew this was exactly what I needed, wanted and yet had fought my entire life. I needed to be her property. I smiled. Finally, the rage was subsiding. The continuous pain I had felt my entire life was fading. I was finally where I belonged. No ordinary man should feel this way.

I was not ordinary.

THREE

THE ESCORT SERVICE

The bills were piling up again since I'd quit my second job. I mentioned this to Athena one day, curious what she meant when she told me, "We'll talk about the money later." She gave me a wicked and mischievous smile, which made me seriously anxious, then handed me a pamphlet from a "dating agency."

"This will be your new job. I've made an appointment for you."

I read the pamphlet for a dating agency called "The One." It clearly stated that they were a dating agency, matching people to possible mates.

I said to her, "How will I get a job working for a dating agency?"

She smiled and replied, "It's a façade. It's an escort agency and you'll be an escort. I've explained your situation to a friend of mine that owns the agency. You've got an appointment tomorrow. We'll go there and my friend will help you get started."

I was quiet, not sure what to say. This wasn't what I wanted but I got the distinct impression that didn't matter, so I said nothing.

The next day, I went to Athena's apartment after work. She showed me the slacks and shirt she had purchased and wanted me to wear, along with a pair of dress shoes. She had completed my questionnaire for the service, and went over the responses I'd give to the set of questions I would be asked during the intake process.

I told her, "I don't like this idea; it's not what I had in mind at all."

Athena looked at me directly and said, "Do you really think you have a choice?"

Silently I realized, no, I didn't have any choice. I was her property. She was enjoying this immensely.

Athena drove me to the agency and after completing paperwork, answering questions for what seemed like several hours and having my picture taken, I was in. They told me to wait at home for a call. The agency charged their clients an initial $4500 consultation fee. Once the client passed the screening process, each date was $500 for the first two hours and then if the date overran, it was an additional $200 for each hour. I'd get $50.00 an hour regardless. The agency made it very clear that they wanted me to encourage the dates to go as long as possible to drive up the tab, and to do whatever it took to make the client happy.

I left the office with the female manager copping a quick feel of my ass as I walked away. Athena told me she was excited for me in this new "job" and that she was sure this will be more to my liking, and definitely much more profitable.

I didn't reply. I didn't like this idea. Something was different about me and I couldn't quite explain it. Before I met her, I would have laughed at the idea of being an escort. To make $50.00 an hour entertaining women who can't get a date would have been laughable to me. Now, however, I felt different. I wasn't sure how but I knew there was something different in the way I saw things.

The first call came the next day. I was required to meet a woman at Chili's restaurant on the south side of the city. She was a lawyer, a prosecuting attorney for the county bordering the one we lived in and she required extreme discretion. I agreed to meet her and planned to show up early to get set mentally for this "date."

I called Athena to tell her about the date, and she replied how happy she was for me and that she hoped this would work out. She ended the call with a cheerful, "Have fun," and hung up. I felt hollow, having hoped she'd tell me not to go, perhaps ask me to quit and come over to wash her car. Hard to believe how far I had fallen in such a short period of time.

I arrived at the Chili's restaurant early to think, sitting down in a booth and ordering a margarita and chips. The time was flying by and before I realized it, the "date" had arrived. She was pretty, smart, and interesting to talk to. The two hours flew by and then three.

Finally she said, "Would you like to come to my apartment for some drinks?"

I thought this over; I suppose the answer she expected was "yes" or "of course."

The answer I gave her was, "I'm afraid not."

Abruptly she changed from smiling, cheerful and playfully flirting with me to stern, serious and emotionless. She was angry but didn't make a scene.

"May I ask why? I've paid for this time and your services. This isn't cheap and I expect certain benefits for the price I paid. No one has ever said no to my invitation before."

I tried to explain and finally it came to me as I fumbled around in my head, juggling the strange new feelings and emotions I now felt daily.

In the end I told her this, "I'm unable to go to your apartment because, as strange as it sounds, I'm the property of another woman. She doesn't love me, but I'm irrevocably hers and without her expressed permission, I can't be with anyone else."

The attorney erupted in an angry whisper stating, "That is the biggest crock of shit I've ever fucking heard. You will come to my apartment and do what the fuck I ask, or I will see you're fired!"

"I'm sorry but that's the truth."

I got up and left the restaurant, leaving the furious and humiliated attorney in the booth.

I drove around for a while, trying to think what I would tell Athena. My cell phone rang; the agency was calling to ask what had gone wrong. The client was very upset. They quickly fired me and reminded me of the agreement I had signed about never discussing the agency with anyone. A threat was implied in that conversation and again, I understood how far I had fallen. Now escort services felt they could threaten me, hard up attorneys looked at me as a fuck toy and here I was, worried about how I would explain to Athena why I couldn't work the fifty dollar an hour job she had signed me up for. The fact I cared so deeply what Athena thought was a mystery to me. The depth of this need to be hers never ceased to amaze me. It felt shameful and amazing at the same time.

Finally, after a couple of hours of aimless driving, I went home and to bed.

The next day, I was supposed to go to Athena's apartment for dinner, and I would have to tell her what had happened. The day flew by. Weird how when I don't want the time to pass quickly, it flies by. I needed time to think and it seemed the day was on meth, streaking past at light speed, edgy and nervous. I was off work well before I was ready and finally called her, telling her I'd be on my way and that I needed to speak about some things.

She said, "Sure, we'll talk when you get here. The door is unlocked, so come in when you get here."

I arrived at her apartment building and knocked on the door, in spite of her permission to enter. She said to come in.

When I walked in, she asked me, "Would you like something to drink?"

I said, "Yes, water."

She nodded and pointed at the cabinet.

"The glasses are in there. Get a drink and then tell me about your "date."

I nodded, it was clear again. Athena served no one when it didn't suit her. I got the glass and filled it with water. Sitting down again at different ends of the couch, I faced forward, anxious about the conversation we were about to have. She told me to look at her and explain what had happened, and warned me to tell her everything, leaving nothing out.

I described what had happened, that I met the attorney, we talked and she was a beautiful woman, smart and strong, but I couldn't do what she wanted. I was not her property, I belonged to you. I explained how angry she was, that I left and was fired a short time later by the agency. When I finished, I searched her face for some hint of what she was thinking. There was nothing there, not a suggestion of what ran through her mind.

The apartment was silent, and finally she said quietly, "Is that all?"

I said, "Yes."

Then louder she said, "Is this what happened?"

I thought she was talking to me, but I heard a woman's voice answer from the hallway, "Yes, it is what happened. He left nothing out."

I heard movement in the hall and immediately jumped to my feet, ready, surprised and not sure what to expect. I didn't know anyone else was in the apartment. A woman walked into the living room and turned to face me.

She smiled and said, "Remember me?"

It was the attorney I had met at Chili's the day before. Athena told me to sit down and began to explain.

"We're friends, as you can see. We've both used the service before to obtain 'dates.'"

I sat back and listened as they outlined the test Athena had laid out for me.

She said, "I wanted to know exactly where your threshold lies in the feeling of ownership. How deep does it really go when faced with a domineering, beautiful, successful, and strong woman? Would you take the opportunity to be owned by anyone, or did you truly feel you belonged to me?"

I was silent sitting on the couch, holding my glass of water, unable to hide the involuntary trembling in my hands. I hoped she understood what I felt, because my actions still baffled me.

Athena and the attorney talked and laughed for a few minutes in the kitchen, then Athena said, "Edge, bring the bottle of Waxed Bat from the fridge and pour each of us a glass of wine."

I got up and found the bottle of wine in the fridge, opened it, and poured three glasses. I brought each of them a glass and then returned with mine. They walked to the living room and sat down, each staring at me in silence, sipping the wine and watching my every move. I waited and watched them staring at me, the way really big cats in the zoo look at you when you walk past their cages. They pace back and forth, looking for a way out and stare at you hungrily, fully aware they could dismember you if it were not for the cage. The look on the two women's faces was intoxicating. I couldn't tear my eyes away.

Finally Athena said, "My friend has spent quite a bit of money to show me what you are truly made of, Edge. I think she needs to be properly thanked, don't you? I'm telling you to serve her as she sees fit. Do whatever she asks. Is that clear?"

It was very clear, and my heart was pounding. Athena understood me much better than I understood myself. She told me to finish my wine, and I followed every detail of the attorney's instructions while Athena watched.

It was hard to remember every detail exactly as the emotions were so intense. The physical really didn't matter. I do remember tasting wine trickling past my lips as I went down on her. I do remember hearing my own voice saying, "Please, don't stop," as she arched her back, pulling me into her as hard as she could. When she was done, she pushed me away. She didn't care about my needs or what I thought. The immediate disconnect was a brutal reminder that she was finished with me. She got up, dressed, and Athena walked her to the door, thanking her and bidding her goodnight.

She then turned to me and said, "Well, you've had an interesting couple of days, haven't you?"

I said quietly, "I suppose, yes."

We cleaned up the glasses and talked for a few minutes.

Finally, Athena said, "Go home, you've given me much to think about."

Just like that, I was dismissed, so I left.

FOUR

PEELING BACK THE ONION

It was a rare day off. I had nothing to do and was getting ready to go to the pool, swim a few laps, and lay out in the hot midday sun. There were few people at the pool in the middle of the day and it was quiet. The water felt amazing in the midday heat as I started cranking out the laps. A quarter of a mile later, I got out refreshed, recharged, and breathing hard.

I checked my phone and found a missed call. Athena had rung and left a message. She was coming to my place on her lunch hour and wanted to know where I was. I texted her saying I was at the pool and just as I sent it, she called to me from the locked entrance to the pool area.

After letting her into the pool area, she said, "So, this is where you live. It's quiet."

I replied, "Yes, that's why I chose it. I need the quiet, the peace, and silence."

Again, everything I said was evaluated and analyzed. She watched me, taking it all in. Maybe because we were on my home turf, or maybe because I was feeling better, I wasn't sure which, but I decided to challenge her on recent developments.

"Why the constant testing and watching my reactions? It seems as if you're looking for a reason not to believe what you see, that I am what I am."

Athena raised her eyebrows at this question and said nothing, but watched everything. I stared back and waited. Several minutes passed and still no reply. She seemed tired, suddenly very tired, edgy and frayed at the seams.

Suddenly, I had an epiphany and said, "Today is Friday, why don't you come over here tonight and let me make you dinner? We could watch a movie, talk, or just chill. You've never seen my condo and I'd like you to feel comfortable there. Please, consider it."

Athena started to say no, she had plans, and then said, "You know, I could come over afterward..."

She stopped mid-sentence, allowing me to jump in saying, "Yes! Afterward then."

I smiled to myself and she announced she had to leave. She got up and I walked her to the gate, unlocking it and saying, "See you tonight!"

She said, "Sure, see you then, Edge."

I watched her walk away, my eyes heavy as I took in her curves and the suggestive sway of her hips. It was an amazing sight. Swimming a few more laps, I felt elated and excited at the possibility she'd come to my condo. Every meeting had been on her terms or at her place, with her setting the stage for another test, another session of pushing my buttons and watching my reactions. I wondered how this might change meeting at my place. Will the where and when we meet change the dynamic between us? We would see.

The rest of the day was spent cleaning my condo, picking out what to make for dinner, what wine to drink, and what music to play. I wanted the moment to be perfect. I eat totally different to most people. I eat very clean, simple food. Healthy, low fat, high protein meals. I picked out two large boneless, skinless chicken breasts, and paired the meat with young tender asparagus shoots. The meal would be simple but flavorful, and I complemented it with a bottle of her favorite wine, Ravenswood Zinfandel. I seasoned the meat lightly with Lawrey's season salt and it was all ready to go.

Next, I picked out the music, going to an old favorite of mine, opera. After sifting through several choices, I pulled out a single piece I have always liked: Mozart's "The marriage of Figaro, Sull Aria." It is a duet and one of the most amazing pieces I have ever heard. I planned on following that up with Schubert's "Avai Maria." I prefer the version by Georgia

Odett. The rest of the night was spent making sure that everything was perfect. This may be the one and only time Athena came to my place, so I planned on making the most of it.

Later that night, I was still waiting and nothing. No call, no message. Finally, at 8:30 I texted her and asked if she was still coming. The response was immediate, and she would be at my place in a few minutes. Three minutes later, she knocked on the door. The timing seemed curious. Had she been sitting outside watching, waiting for me to contact her, always maintaining the upper hand? I didn't know.

Regardless, I started dinner and poured her a glass of wine. Athena walked quietly around my house, looking at pictures and pulling books off the shelves. She absorbed everything, watched everything.

Finally, dinner was ready and we sat down to eat. I have to admit, I make the best chicken you will ever eat so I sat back and watched her reaction as she tasted the first bite. She tried to hide her surprise, but obviously she liked it. I smiled at how she tried not to show how much she enjoyed my simple cooking. Athena is a gourmet chef, every dish is perfect and amazing. I, on the other hand, am a simple cook. I keep it simple and clean. Healthy is what I strive for first, closely followed by flavorful.

After dinner, which she ate completely, we went for a short walk outside. Athena was silent at first but finally said, "It's so peaceful here. You live in the middle of the city and yet it's so amazingly quiet!"

I told her again, "That's why I moved here."

She started to relax and noticeably her shoulders became less tense, her smile was more genuine. Again, I noticed how tired she looked and incredibly worn out. I started to ask her a question and stopped.

She said, "Finish the question you were about to ask."

I replied, "It's not my place to ask something like this."

She said, "I'm making it your place, so ask."

I paused and considered how to phrase the question. Finally, I said, "You look incredibly tired. Do you sleep well, or, for that matter, at all?"

Her face tightened and hardened, and for a moment I thought, *Fuck, I ruined the whole night with one stupid question.*

Finally, she said, "I think I'll stay here tonight. That's fine with you, isn't it?"

It was a question and yet not a question, more a statement. I was always amazed how she did that, ask a question in a way that was a demand.

I replied, "If that's what you'd like to do. Yes, you're always welcome."

An hour or so later, we were lying in bed. After her usual intense, dominant sexual demands, we were both spent, sweat glistening on our bodies. She said good night and rolled over, falling asleep quickly while I lay there, listening to her slow rhythmic breathing. Sleep never came easy for me.

An hour later, I was just starting to nod off when she began dreaming. At first, she made little twitching movements, small involuntary jerks of a foot or knee. I smiled at the childlike movements she made. Soon however, the movements became less childlike and more frantic. The dreams lost their childlike innocence. Athena was in a battle for her life, crying out, thrashing about, afraid, and alone. The transformation was heartbreaking. I tried to wake her and she wouldn't open her eyes. My hand on her shoulder was woven into the dream and she abruptly shoved it away.

She said, "Get your fucking hands off me."

I apologized and got no response, realizing she was still locked into the nightmarish grip of the dream. A few more minutes of this and I'd had enough, I couldn't sit by and watch while she was so tormented. I pulled her to me firmly as her fighting became more frantic. Finally, she woke up with several short gasps, looking around wildly and then remembering where she was.

I said, "You were dreaming. It's over now, you're okay, I'm here. Lay your head down and rest."

She looked at me, vulnerable and angry, ashamed I have seen this side of her.

Again, drawing out the word, I said, "Rest."

She laid her head on my shoulder, immediately falling asleep. I'd like to say she slept soundly and peacefully for the rest of the night. However, that didn't happen. There were three more nightmares of similar intensity, ending with a similar result. Each time, I coaxed her back to sleep and she dropped off immediately.

The reason for her incredible fatigue was obvious now. We all have our demons and after a night of seeing hers, I now understood the reason for the constant tests, watching for my reaction. I didn't sleep much her first night at my place. I watched over her, stopping the dreams before she became too entrapped in them, coaxing her back to sleep.

Finally at 8:00 a.m., I got up and had breakfast. I checked on her, watching her sleep, making sure she was okay. Eventually at noon, she woke up, rolling over.

"Morning. I see you're up already, Edge."

I replied, "I've been up for several hours."

"Oh? Do you have insomnia too?"

"Yes, occasionally I actually sleep. It's rare but I can't ever sleep in. I have to get up."

She said, "Sleep in? What do you mean sleep in, what time is it?"

I replied, "It's noon. You've been asleep for fourteen hours."

Athena just stared at me and said quietly, "Are you serious?"

"Yes, it's noon. Would you like breakfast or lunch?"

She looked at her phone on the nightstand in disbelief.

"Noon!" Lying back she said, "I feel amazing. I can't remember the last time I slept that well."

It was my turn to watch and learn.

I said, "Yes, you fell asleep rather quickly."

Leaving out the horrific nightmares and frantic battles she fought in her dreams. She laid back and smiled at me, a look of complete satisfaction on her face.

She said, "Can I have some black coffee and maybe toast?"

"Sure, I'll get it brewing. Do you want it here in bed or downstairs?"

"No, I'll be down in a minute. I want to get up."

She remembered nothing from the night, none of the dreams, nothing she had said or done. Apparently, we both needed each other but for different reasons. Peeling back the layers of the onion was always an enlightening experience. We each had our emotional baggage and needed this relationship, but for different reasons.

I went downstairs and prepared to grind up the coffee. New Mexico Pinion coffee is my favorite brand. It is excellent black and freshly ground. After the coffee finished brewing and her toast and jelly was out on the table, I called upstairs to her to let her know it was ready. She came downstairs freshly showered, wearing one of my shirts and nothing else.

I wondered how this day would end as she commented again, "Your house is so incredibly quiet, and this coffee! What brand is this?"

Smiling, I told her about the coffee.

Then she said as she took a bite of the toast, "I don't remember the last time I felt this much at peace—" Athena stopped mid-sentence and said, "Oh my god! What kind of bread is this? It's the best I've ever eaten."

I explained it was my favorite brand, Alpine Harvest Multi-Grain. It was organic and really very good.

I watched her for some sign of sarcasm, anything that would let me know she was being guarded. Nothing was there. She really felt safe, maybe for the first time in ages.

I heard a distant and quiet voice saying, "You could move in." Then a long pause. "I mean, I'd like it if you chose to stay here. If you wanted to."

Feeling hot and flushed, I realized my embarrassment and slight terror. I looked down at my coffee and waited for the laughter at such a ridiculous idea. Athena would never move in with me. No laughter came.

Finally, a firm voice said, "Yes, I'd like that. I'll move in immediately." I couldn't believe it, and was unable to look up from my coffee.

Finally, she said, "Edge, did you hear me? I'll start moving in tonight. I'll need a key."

I got up immediately, went to the kitchen, and opened a drawer where I kept miscellaneous items. I call it the junk drawer. I pulled out a freshly made key and handed it to her. She looked at the key, still attached to a tag from the locksmith, running her fingers up and down the freshly cut edges.

"When did you have this key made?"

I replied, "Yesterday."

"Why did you have a key made for me? Did you assume I would want to move in with you?"

"No, I made you a key because you own me. To continue to deny you access to my home feels wrong, I can't do it anymore."

She said nothing, sipping her coffee and watching me. Finally she replied, "Yes, that's how it should be. Now, about your bills. How much money do you need to make up for the job I told you to quit?"

FIVE

A LIFE TRANSFORMED

A few months later, my life has been turned upside down. I still lived in the condo in the same quiet neighborhood, surrounded by older retired people and I was the youngest person in the community by a couple of decades. I spent as much time at the outdoor pool as I could, swimming and laying in the sun. The community was quiet, and the neighbors mostly minded their own business.

Athena moved into the condo about five months after riding me under the desk. I didn't know if she still saw other men or not, and I didn't care. She had moved in, that was all that mattered. Occasionally, she had to attend social functions and meetings with other officers. The meetings were a thinly veiled excuse to drink and mingle with her peer group. I was sure that while she was there "mingling," other men and woman were thinking they'd like to get together with her. She was that kind of woman. No matter what room she entered, no matter what the crowd or social circle, the sexual attraction that surrounded her affected everyone present.

Anyway, tonight I had to work a late shift and I wouldn't be home until after midnight. She phoned me and said she had another function to go to, one she called the CGOC meeting. I asked what CGOC stood for. She told me it was short for Company Grade Officers Club. Athena had recently been awarded the CGOC of the year award and was expected to be at every event they hosted. She said she would be late coming home and that we'd probably arrive about the same time back at the condo. She hung up, and I wondered what really went on at these meetings. Images filled my head. Athena had turned my world upside down.

She had a couple of months left in the military and had basically thrown caution to the wind. I had been under her desk more times than I could remember now, and heard more male and female voices in conversations with her about dates, sexual encounters, and the things she has done with them. She laughed about meeting one guy in a house that was under construction at lunchtime. They had sex in one of the back bedrooms and the construction crew came in to work on the house. She giggled, recalling they barely got dressed in time before the crew came into the room. The man she'd fucked in the house was laughing as well while I was under the desk, her hands gently grinding my face against her wet clit while they talked. It was an amazing feeling to be so unconditionally owned like this. I had dreamed about it for so long, I couldn't remember thinking any other way.

I finally made it home the night of the meeting and there was no one home. I changed out of my uniform, and put the bulletproof vest and leather gear I have to wear in the closet. After showering the days sweat off me, I got dressed.

I heard talking downstairs, and recognized Athena plus two other voices. She called out to me that she was home. Athena had changed the entire appearance of the condo since she moved in. All of the appliances had been replaced with new stainless steel designer ones. Hardwood floors now covered the entire main floor, replacing the worn carpet. There was new paint and furniture throughout the home. The transformation of the condo was as substantial as the effect she'd had on my life. We were both different now, better than before. That was the influence she seemed to have everywhere she went. Everything just got better. If you could handle the complexity of who she was, you got on better right along with her.

I came down the stairs and met her with two other junior grade officers she had invited to the condo. She introduced us and asked me to take the guests' coats, which I did. Athena had introduced the woman as Bjanna and the man as Zeke; they were each a first lieutenant and had been dating for about six months. I picked up on the details of their relationship as I brought them all a beer and some small snacks to eat, cold cuts and crackers with her favorite cheese, Havarti. Eventually, they all settled in and I took a seat next to Athena.

Bjanna asked how long we had been together.

Athena looked at me and said, "About two or three months I guess."

Zeke asked her where we met.

Athena said, "Oh, we met on the gate at the base. I caught him looking up my skirt one day and confronted him about it."

The room was silent.

Zeke said, "Are you serious?"

Athena answered, "Of course! You don't make shit like that up!"

"Wow, I thought you'd have had him fired for that."

"Oh, I almost did, actually. I called him into my office and had decided to fire him when it occurred to me there might be a better use for him."

Bjanna said, "Oh really, and what was that?"

Athena smiled and said, "He's my property now. I own his ass and it's just what he wants. I forced him under my desk and made him go down on me my while I worked."

They both looked at her and me. Finally, Zeke said, "Bullshit. I mean no disrespect, Captain, but you don't really mean that do you?"

"Yes, I do. Whenever I call him, he spends lunch under my desk like the good little bitch he is, licking my pussy and ass, and he loves it!"

"And people don't catch you?"

"No! Not yet at least."

He laughed and said, "That is awesome! Holy fucking shit, it's like something you read in Penthouse Forum."

"Well, he does what I tell him, when I tell him. I own him, it works out perfectly."

I had said nothing during this exchange. It was all true. There was not much more I could do except offer them another beer. They both accepted, quiet now, and finally noticed I had served her every need the entire time they were present. The reality of what she had told them set in.

Bjanna said, "I was in your office last week. Was he under the desk then?"

Athena was quiet for a moment, and then said, "What day was that?"

"Wednesday, at about eleven forty-five?"

"Yes he was, he had been for about fifteen minutes by then."

Bjanna smiled and said, "Wow, I thought you looked flushed and happier than normal. I just thought you have a great lunch hour."

Athena said, "Oh, I did have a great lunch hour. I had sex with Captain Ching at his apartment and then called my little bitch boy here to finish."

The two officers were speechless at this disclosure.

Finally Zeke said, "Yeah, I heard Captain Ching saying that he was dating you but I didn't want to say anything. Now it makes sense to me. You were, or should I say, are seeing him and yet you live with this guy." He motioned to me.

Athena said, "It's not that complicated. I see whomever I wish, whenever I wish. Edge here is my property, I own him. Simple as that."

The tension in the room was thick.

Finally, Bjanna said, "Captain, is this some kind of prank? No one owns anyone like that, so unconditionally."

Athena said, "I do."

Zeke said in a defiant tone, "Prove it then."

Athena said to me, "No one believes I own you, bitch. Guess you're going to have to prove it. Get down on your knees in front of my chair, and remove my pants."

I did as she asked without hesitation. She spread her legs and threw one leg over my shoulder.

"Do what you were born to do, bitch, dive in."

I went down on her while the two junior officers laughed loud, heartily, and long.

"Jesus, he really is your property!" said Zeke.

I stayed there for about twenty minutes until she finally came, hips pumping as she rode me. She got up, pulled her pants back on and said to the two mesmerized officers, "See, I told you. Property!"

I stood and she said, "Go wash your face, and come back with another beer for each of us."

I did what she said, silently. Returning to the room a few minutes later, I found the conversation had changed. My status as Athena's property was no longer in question and was accepted as fact. They stayed another hour or so and finally left. I asked Athena if she thought they would give her secret away.

She said, "No they won't. They're both married to other people and have been seeing each other on the side for some time. They won't violate my trust as I haven't violated theirs."

The next time I was under the desk, I heard Athena talking to Bjanna. She had come into the office just as I started to go down on her. They chatted for a few moments then Bjanna said quietly, "He's under your desk right now, isn't he?"

Athena said, "Where he belongs, yes!"

Bjanna laughed a mischievous laugh and said, "Can I look?"

"Of course."

She leaned back in her chair, exposing my face buried between her legs. Bjanna laughed again. "Where can I find a man like that?"

"Well, I found this one at the west gate trying to look up my skirt."

They both chuckled while I enthusiastically continued under the desk, doing what I was born to do.

SIX

THE O CLUB

Another week of checking IDs at the gate was about to come to an end. I was happy to be off work. The seasons were changing and the mornings were cool, but the afternoons warmed up to a comfortable temperature. I planned on going swimming that night while Athena attended another CGOC meeting. I was on my way home when she called, asking me to pick her up at the Officers' Club. She said she'd had too much to drink and needed a ride home. I was pleased she asked me to help her, and gladly turned my old Ford truck around and headed back to the base. The Officers' Club was on the other side of the base and wasn't a place I was familiar with. When I arrived, I texted her to say I was outside when she was ready.

I waited for several minutes with no reply. Nothing. I looked inside the building from my truck and didn't see her. Finally, she replied, "Come inside. Take the hallway on the left and meet me at the third door on the left."

I read the text again. Really? I texted back to say I was still in uniform. Couldn't she just come out? She replied, "Perfect. I'll be waiting for you."

Sighing, I shut off the truck's engine. She must be really drunk, she rarely texted and usually didn't want others to see us together, especially when I was in my uniform. Gate guards are considered the lowest of the contractors working on the base, in spite of the fact they are some of the highest paid employees. Status is everything to these idiots and I laughed to myself as I entered the club, wondering what they would think as I left with the officer who just won the award for the best company grade officer of the year. I was sure these arrogant fucks would be talking shit. The thought of it made me smile. I may have become her property, but my dislike for officers, especially female officers, hadn't waned a bit.

As I walked up to the glass doors, which are the main entrance to the O Club, I saw a woman inside watching me. As I approached the door, she did as well.

"May I help you?"

Her tone implied, "What do you think you are doing here?"

I said, "No, I don't think you can help me at all."

Meaning, "Fuck off you snotty, arrogant little self-important bitch."

I pressed on and ignored her, taking the left hallway and at the third door, I stopped and reached to open it. Then I felt Athena's hand on my shoulder. She was behind me.

"Hey you!"

I looked down the hallway and the "greeter" was gone. No one was present in the hallway except us. Athena was noticeably intoxicated and I asked if she was ready to go.

She said, "Yes, but I have one small favor to ask of you."

She turned me around, facing away from her.

"I found this in a box of all your cop stuff and thought it had possibilities."

As she said this, she slipped something around my neck and tightened it. I assumed it was a collar of some kind, and it was, but not just any collar.

Like I said before, I used to be a cop and was awarded an assignment to the K-9 unit, handling a German Shepherd who was the single most stubborn dog I have ever met. I had to use an electronic shock collar to get him to do the simplest tasks. The other handlers found his moodiness hilarious and he was a constant embarrassment to me. When I left the unit after several years as a handler, I put the electronic collar away. Apparently, Athena had found it, and a use for it.

She secured the collar and had me turn around, making sure it fit snugly. Then she tested the collars warning mode to let me know it was indeed charged and ready to go. I felt the *bzzz* as she activated the hand held remote. Suddenly, she didn't seem so drunk.

She said, "There now, come with me," and pushed the remote, warning me again.

We walked past the third door and the fifth, to the last one in the hallway. A sign on the door said, "Do Not Disturb, Meeting in Progress." Athena opened it and walked in, with me following nervously. The room we entered was a conference room. There were tables set up in a U-shape and chairs at each table. It was your basic meeting room, except for the refreshment bar and a table with small sandwiches set out on several plates. The meeting had not yet started. Apparently, they were waiting for me.

Athena walked me to the front and took off my jacket. The room was filled with female officers. The same uppity bitch I had basically told to fuck off as I entered the club was there, as were several others I had discreetly "Yes ma'amed" at one time or another. However, the reality of my tone of voice and non-verbal communication was less than respectful. They all watched and laughed quietly as Athena started to speak.

"Apparently, word of my property has got around the base and some of you have asked me questions about him. I have agreed to make him available to members of the club tonight only. You'll see for yourselves the level of ownership I have over him and I have told him he will serve you, if you wish."

I was in serious shit.

A room full of angry entitled bitches looked at me, and I had an electric shock collar strapped to my neck.

Athena said to me quietly, "We'll see how deep your need to serve me goes tonight, Edge. I was impressed by your response at the escort agency, but this is another type of test entirely. Let's see how you do."

She walked across the room to the same snotty little bitch that had confronted me at the door of the club, and handed her the remote.

I heard Athena say, "He's yours."

An evil smile crossed the woman's face and she pushed the red button. Lightning shot through my neck and face, I cried out involuntarily.

She smiled and said, "I see it does work. Now do you understand without question what will happen if you don't do exactly as I say?"

I replied quietly "Yes."

"Louder, or you will ride the lightning again. Keep in mind, gate guard, that was the first setting. There are five more."

I replied quickly and louder, "Yes!"

She forced me to my knees, handcuffed with my own cuffs. I had to perform for the snotty bitch until she was satisfied. She belittled me the entire time, reminding me of every time I had disrespected her.

She then said, "Look at me while you suck on my clit, you arrogant ass!"

I had to look up at her while I did everything she asked, without hesitation. When she finally finished with me, she passed the remote to another woman. I recognized faces and remembered conversations I'd had with each of them. I was forced to do whatever they wanted and if I didn't meet their expectations, the collar would let me know.

It was compulsory to lick every ass in the room. I was stripped and laughed at while standing naked in the middle of the room. My erect cock was measured and that too was ridiculed. Pictures were taken of me in every humiliating position you can imagine. One woman had brought a crop whip and wanted me to take a blow from everyone in the room. The women eagerly lined up and struck me repeatedly, on the face, chest, back, balls...no place was left unpunished on my body.

Athena watched it all quietly from the corner, gauging my reaction to every demand. When it had finished, I was bruised, bitten, fucked, scratched, slapped, and humiliated. One woman put a dog leash on the collar and made me crawl on the floor, parading me around. Every female officer on base that was present had come in my face. Several had taken pictures for their friends while I submitted to whatever they asked.

Then finally, it was over. They all left and Athena brought me my clothes and released me from the handcuffs. She told me to get dressed and keep the collar on. I did what she said. My head was swimming, the reality of the way I had been used and violated was seeping in, and I stumbled as I tried to get dressed.

As I struggled to stand up, I heard her say, "Are you okay? Do you need a drink of water?" I shook my head and she said, "Then breathe deep. Catch your breath, Edge."

I did as she said and finally my head started to clear.

"How do you feel?"

How did I feel? I thought about it, not sure what to tell her.

"Are you sure you want to know what I feel?"

She stood in front of me and said, "Look at me and tell me how you feel."

I was in conflict. I felt humiliated and angry, while at the same time I was high on endorphins. I could hardly keep my eyes open.

I managed to tell her, "I feel like I'm high on some kind of drug. You'll have to drive us home."

Athena stared at me and only said, "Interesting."

She drove me home and walked me upstairs, helping me get into bed. I slept more soundly than I have in years.

Traffic increased in my lane dramatically after that day. The women officers came in, smiling knowing smiles. Some made comments, and others laughed as they passed by. The secret was out. Every one of them knew it. I was unquestionably Athena's property and she had shared me with each and every one of them.

SEVEN

THE ADULT POOL

A s I told you before, the condo complex where I lived had swimming pools, one for the kids and their parents, and one for the adults. That basically meant the adult pool was for people who didn't like children. Most of the people who lived in the complex had grandkids and went to the kids' pool. It was the pool I preferred as well. Watching the kids play Marco Polo or dive for toys in the deep end was a constant source of entertainment. Occasionally, the kids' pool would have an issue; the heater would break, or the chlorine content would become too high and then the crowd would switch to the adult pool until it was fixed. That was what brought us to the adult pool this week.

The heater had been out for a few days and the water was cold in the kids' pool. We went there every chance we got and so when the time came, we headed to the adult pool. It was quieter than usual and there was no one there when we arrived. I tested the water and it was warm. Several condominiums overlooked the cement pool and surrounding lounge area, and people were frequently in the windows watching us as we got ready to swim. Athena noticed our audience and smiled. She didn't say much but I saw a mischievous look in her eye.

She went about her normal routine of setting up a chair to lie on after she got out of the water. Putting the latest book she was reading on the towel, she laid it across the chair, marking it as hers. She sat in the chair, ensuring she faced the majority of condominium windows fronting the pool, and widely spread her legs as she removed her sandals. Then, she ran her hands up each leg until her fingers were on the white bikini panties that barely existed between her legs, rubbing her pussy two or three times and making a few little circles with her fingers. Athena left no doubt to any of the would-be-spectators that they needed to keep watching, for this would be a show they'd remember for many days to come. She ran both hands up her abdomen towards her breasts, and gently rubbed them until her nipples were hard.

Athena lay back and warmed herself in the hot sun, smiling to herself. I imagined she was weighing her options of what to do next. I watched all of this from the water, wondering how many of the phones were ringing right now as the neighbors called each other, increasing her audience. The older people were like that, they had a network. I swam laps while Athena warmed herself and stretched like a cat in the sun. She rolled onto her front and pulled the sides of her bikini bottoms deep into the crack of her ass, spreading her legs slightly. I imagined a few hearts were pounding at that move.

Finally, I got out and sat next to her for a moment, starting to get warm, when three men and one woman entered the patio from the opposite side we were sitting. They were all in their mid-twenties, fit and tanned, and had a target lock on the sight of Athena's perfect ass browning in the sun. She turned and looked at each one, sizing up the audience she was about to entertain then put her head back down and continued to warm in the sun. Eventually, she got up and stretched, inviting me to join her in the water in her usual fashion.

"Edge, join me in the pool."

It was not a request.

The three men watched intently as did the woman, while Athena slipped seductively into the water. I joined her and she swam around for a moment until she stopped strategically, sitting on the stairs across from the group of watchers both on the patio and in the surrounding windows.

She said to me with a seductive smile, "Edge, come sit by me."

I swam underwater from across the pool and as I got closer, she removed her bikini panties underwater. I stayed down there a few more moments and swam right up to her spread legs, licking her smooth pussy underwater before coming up between her legs into the air.

She said, "The water feels amazing, doesn't it?"

I barely noticed. She had both hands inside my suit, gently touching me and encouraging my already erect cock.

"Too bad there are so many people here, Edge. I'd love you to lick my ass on the side of the pool after you fuck me in the water."

I loved the idea. We kissed for a while and explored each other in the water while the audience watched. I lifted her up, nearly out the water and sat on the stairs behind her.

She slipped off my trunks and said quietly, "Fuck me right now, in front of these people."

At first, she was discreet while I slipped inside her in the warm water. It was noon and the sun beat down on us while we moved rhythmically. The pool was a calm surface as we started, glass-like and smooth. I was sure the group of watchers had a clear view of her spread legs and my cock inside her. She grabbed me frantically and kissed me over her shoulder.

"Oh God, this turns me on so much, Edge, don't stop."

The waves of the pool gained in size as we moved faster and faster under the surface. Her fingernails dug into my legs over and over, trying to drive me deeper inside her. Finally, we both came and she cried out, breathing deeply. Not one of the watchers on the patio said a word. The men and women just watched mesmerized, as we both pulled our swimsuits back on under the water and started to swim across the pool towards our chairs. One of the men leaned in and whispered to the woman. As we got out of the pool, they got in and swam around. They were obviously trying to work up the courage to have sex in the pool. It never went further than kissing and heavy petting. Athena and I watched as we warmed in the sun.

She said to me, "Would you put some baby oil on my legs?" and handed me the bottle.

She had me start at her feet, carefully working my way up her legs. As I added oil, the couple got out of the water. The woman was obviously frustrated and angry at the lack of adventurousness her man had displayed. Athena smiled as I worked the oil into her thighs and made a deep "*mmmmm*" noise.

"I want you to oil me up, Edge."

She pulled her bikini panties to one side and began to grind her hips against my hand, guiding me, forcing my fingers inside her, first one finger, then two and then three as her need deepened. She took deep breaths, making small animal-like noises of intense pleasure and no secret of what she was doing as the group watched attentively. Eventually, she slowed down her gyrations and opened her eyes, smiling.

"That was nice," she said. "Now put oil on the rest on me."

She left the panties to one side, clearly meaning to perform for her audience. Athena smiled and stretched cat-like, knowing she had everyone's complete attention. She picked up the book she had brought and read. Across the pool, the tension was thick in the group of watchers. The woman was upset that no one paid her any attention. She became more and more frustrated and finally got up, storming off and slamming the gate as she left. Athena had this effect on people. Men were attracted to her dominant and confidant manner, women too. Just not that woman.

EIGHT

CO-WORKERS COMING
OVER TONIGHT

A couple of years have passed. Today we live in the mountains in Colorado. Some things have changed, and others have not. I was still her property, no doubt about that. Every day was a reminder that my sole reason for being was to serve her. I made her dinner, cleaned her house, and washed her clothes. I poured the wine she drank and washed the dishes. This was the reality of being owned by someone. You don't just get to do the sexy things. Current books never mention that part of the partnership. They paint a false picture and people apparently like to read that. I tried to read the latest one; I couldn't stomach it. Even though I completely understood the dynamics of the relationship it described, to see a woman in a submissive role wasn't something I could believe in. I have never seen it in the real world. Women are much too smart, and it seems to me they allow the illusion of being controlled to exist to serve their own purpose. Anyway, that's beside the point. I wrote this in my spare time because she wanted me to tell anyone who will read this exactly how she owns me.

I no longer had a job; I quit because she required it. I write when my time is my own and when it wasn't, I literally served her.

I work out in the gym we have in the basement. I have always loved to work out, and she provided me with an amazing weight room and cardio machines to feed that hobby. Athena works out as well, when she isn't working or on a business trip. I have to keep a phone nearby when I work out, in case she calls, which she always does just to check in. Today, while I did cardio on the Stairmaster, she called. I stopped and answered.

She asked how my day was going and we shared small talk for a few minutes. She told me about several business meetings she had attended, and then mentioned that she had invited several of the women that she worked with over tonight for dinner and drinks.

"Edge, I'd like the house to be clean, and dinner to be ready by seven. Select a wine that will pair well with the meal you prepare for us. I'd like to be pleasantly surprised by the food and wine, so that'll be up to you. There'll be four guests and myself. I want you to be fresh from the weight room, groomed, shaven, and dressed nicely to show you off to my guests. Do you understand?"

My heart was pounding. She had tutored me about wine and food pairing when we had guests before. This wasn't new to me, but I never knew what to expect. She enjoyed making plans that kept me guessing and I never knew what to expect, having learned from experience there was no way to predict exactly what mood she was in.

I replied, "I understand."

She said, "Enjoy the rest of your day, Edge." Then she hung up.

Several hours passed and the house was immaculate. I ran to the store and bought a seven-pound prime rib; the wine was ready. It was 5:30 p.m. and she would be home soon. While I went through my workout of weights and calisthenics, I tried not to think about the evening. I attempted to focus on the routine and clear my head. Weighted dips were my favorite at that moment. I finished with three sets of fifteen with a forty-five pound weight chained to my waist, then I headed upstairs and checked on the prime rib. It was cooking nicely. I hit the shower and then dressed for the night. She liked me to wear dark colors, usually black. I picked out black pants and a snug fitting but comfortable shirt, checked myself in the mirror, and then prepared the stereo. Berlioz, "Symphonie Fantastique Opera Fourteen" cued as the starting music for the night, followed by various Baroque pieces. I waited for her to come home.

She finally arrived, followed by two large black Lincoln Navigators. I saw the stickers on the windshield of each car from the window, indicating they were rental cars. The occupants were from out of town then. They would be women I hadn't met before, all powerful intelligent women I assumed, as she usually only associated with like-minded people.

I waited at the front door, and opened it for her and our guests. They entered one by one, talking to each other and handing me their coats or jackets without a word. I hung each of them up carefully, and then pulled out the wine glasses from the cabinets where we kept the crystal. Starting the music, I placed a wine glass near each of the women, careful not to make eye contact with any of them. This was our agreed method of meeting and serving her female coworkers. My role was clear. I obliged by not embarrassing her with idle chitchat. Silently, I moved among them, pouring wine and checking to see if there was anything else she would like. Athena told me that will be all for now, and I returned to prepare the food. When the food was almost cooked, I set the table with our best dining plates and cutlery. Finally, the table was set. I told her the food was ready and she informed her guests.

While they ate, I filled their glasses with wine. No one looked at me, no one said thank you. I barely registered in their minds as they discussed politics, the business trip they went on and issues with the latest contract proposals. It was fascinating to hear the way their minds grasped the intricacies of their business. The sheer intelligence of each woman was as intoxicating as their physical appearance. They were all as beautiful as they were smart.

Athena told me, "That'll be all. Clean up the table."

They returned to the living room, each taking a seat on the overstuffed leather chairs, while I cleaned up the dining room. I opened another bottle of wine, her favorite, Zinfandel, and refilled the already empty glasses. The women were all comfortable now, and glowing from the wine and excellent food. She told me I would be needed again in a few minutes, a signal that I may leave now as they have things to discuss so I went to the top floor of the house to watch television. From there, I heard them laughing about something, and then it was quiet again. I became engrossed in the basketball game I was watching, having been a Bulls fan forever. Derrick Rose was schooling the New York Nicks. Sometime must have passed because I felt a hand on my shoulder and it startled me.

Athena smiled and said, "Dinner was wonderful, thank you. Now stand up."

I did as she demanded and she had me turn around. She took off my shirt and tied a blindfold around my head. My breathing quickened, and I felt my heart pounding. She had used the blindfold before; it meant someone wanted anonymity, or not for me to know what they were doing. It required complete trust, an acknowledgement of her ownership of me in every way imaginable. Athena checked to make sure the blindfold was secure, and then told me to walk with her as she guided me back downstairs. The room she took me to was quiet.

She asked, "Edge, tell me again who owns you."

"You do."

"And what do you mean to me?"

"I am your property," I replied quietly.

The room was silent. I couldn't tell if the other women had left or not. It was so quiet I could hear her breathing. There was a pause.

I heard another voice asking, "How does that make you feel?"

I was startled; at least one of the women was still here.

"It gives me purpose."

The reply came immediately, "Excellent!"

She left me standing there and I now heard movement in the room. Chairs were being moved, but no one spoke. More than one person was there and I tried to determine how many of the women remained. I couldn't tell. Then she was back.

"You'll make me very proud of you, Edge. Do you understand?"

"Yes."

This was not a statement but a command. Athena brought me to a position in the room and I was aware of someone in front of me.

I heard a voice saying, "I'd like him to kneel."

She whispered in my ear, "Kneel, Edge. I'll be right here, watching you the entire time."

I knelt and immediately a hand cupped my head, not pulling me, just supporting me. Before I could take in a breath, I felt a woman pressing her wet pussy against my mouth, grinding slowly at first, her foot resting on my shoulder. This may surprise you, but don't be astonished. It had happened before. I was her property and she shared me with whoever she wished. I had no say in the matter. This was decided long ago under the desk. The grinding and smothering continued until at last, in a final shuddering physical thrust, the woman came in my face. I tasted her cum in my mouth and for a moment, she gasped for air, breathing rapidly.

Then I heard a voice say to her, "You were right, he is quite talented."

Someone wiped a warm wet cloth over my face and I was shared with the next woman, and then the next. Again and again, I was forced to provide the woman with sexual pleasure. Some took more than one turn. I knew because I counted how many times they used me.

I wish I could tell you I didn't like being treated this way. That would be a lie. I didn't care who they were, or what they wanted me to do. Athena wanted to watch me do this and I did as she asked.

I heard one woman say, "I want him to lick me from behind."

She answered, "He'll do anything you ask, that's his place. I own him."

Next, I felt firm buttock cheeks pressed against my face, and I licked and explored the ass and pussy in front of me. The ass began to ride me and a hand grabbed my head, driving me deeper, while another hand pulled the buttocks wider.

I heard Athena say, "Edge, show her how deep you can explore with your tongue."

I did as I was told, and I heard the woman gasp repeatedly, her muscles quivering as she came. This went on for a while, with each woman taking her turn with me. I lost track of how many times to be honest, the feeling was too intense to care about how many times I was used this way.

When they finished with me, Athena placed a hand on my shoulder and said, "You can get up now."

I was breathing hard from the exertion, and my lips were swollen and sore from the hard repetitive grinding. She guided me to our room and removed the blindfold. The lights were dim and my eyes had no problem adjusting.

She said, "You may shower now and go to bed. I'll be in later."

Much later, we were in bed, and the women who used me have left. I'd never know their names, who they were, or where they were from. I didn't know if they were married or single, it didn't matter. All that mattered was that I was owned. I was her property.

She said to me, "I want you to tell me how that felt and why you liked it so much."

I bared my twisted soul to her, and explained that I truly enjoyed being treated this way and why. I wasn't allowed to break eye contact with her while I told her this, it was a rule. Her eyes were ablaze, much like that first time she face fucked me under her desk.

When I finished she said, "I was very proud of you tonight, thank you."

As she turned out the lights, I smiled in the darkness. I was very fortunate she understood me. Most women wouldn't. I slept deeper than I had in months, my darkest needs fulfilled again.

NINE
THE MAJOR'S HOUSE

Sometimes we traveled. Athena worked as a consultant and her job required some travel. I hated it but there were benefits. New places, new people, great restaurants were all positives, but I missed the solitude of home on the mountain. Notice I did not say our home. Although I lived there and Athena told me that it was "ours," it wasn't a concept I could grasp any more. There was no "ours." There was "hers;" the house was hers, the cars were hers, and I was hers. I was nothing more than that. Some of you reading this might find that strange. In reality, this was the safest I have ever felt. There was no mysterious magical force of love that kept us together. This was the reality of her ownership of me, the undeniable fact I was property, like the cars, the house, and weight equipment in the gym downstairs. I served a selfish and one-sided purpose. I was the selfish one, and the one sided purpose was my own. I needed this now more than anything. More than words can ever describe. You would have to see it in action to understand the depth of this need, and maybe even then it isn't possible to grasp.

Anyway, as I said, we were traveling. This trip was going to be good because we were staying at her friend's home, Bliss Wood. I liked Bliss immensely. She was another woman like Athena, a military officer, a Major. They met in the military after 9/11. Friendships born in battle are lifelong,

I suppose and they both played their part, maybe not on the front lines but definitely key roles to make the military machine function at its best. They were both power women, leaders, people that made things happen. It was intoxicating to be in the room and listen to them talk. Actually, it was a bit like a drug. I rarely slept when we stayed at Bliss' home. My head spun, it was hard to concentrate.

I usually made them dinner and picked out the wine while they talked about things they had done and places they had seen. They laughed about old relationships and men they had kicked to the curb. I shuddered at the thought of being one of those men someday, listening and trying not to think about how bad it felt to only be able to make them dinner and wash the dishes when they were finished. This was the most I could hope for. I dared not speak up or ask Athena for more. She knew how this felt for me. She saw my torment and the need to serve them both.

When we went to bed, she said, "I see you're struggling. Would you rather stay somewhere else?"

I said, "No, I like being here."

It was painfully true. Bliss' home was like Athena's: a reflection of the woman and her deepest thoughts. There were maps of the Middle East on the walls, pictures of her in Baghdad, Afghanistan, and all over the world. Bliss traveled a lot; most women who are like this did. Their talents are needed everywhere.

When they both went to work, I was left to wander the house and look at the pictures and maps on the wall. It was an intimate moment, but not in a creepy way. To be able to walk freely in Bliss' home was a gift of trust and I didn't take it lightly. She had no idea of my status, being property, being an object that was owned and used, and needing it to be that way. It felt wrong to hide it from her after seeing her home and being allowed to walk in it freely. They were like sisters, kindred spirits, and I hated the lie of hiding this. It felt like lying to Athena and that is something I wouldn't do.

The first night at Bliss' home, the plan was for me to make blackened fish and asparagus for dinner. I chose a wine to match and got things ready. Bliss was late coming home and Athena decided we would wait for her before I started dinner. She was in a training class, Airborne Jumpmaster School. Imagine that! Told you they were both awesome women. It was hard to think with them both in the same room.

I concentrated on the dinner and tried to clear my head, hoping that I didn't say anything really stupid. Funny thing was, for some reason they both accepted me in spite of their obvious intellectual superiority and drive to excel. They seemed interested in my comments and it was hard to focus on finishing the dinner preparations. Images flashed into my head of what it would be like to serve them both, to be property of each of them, passed back and forth between them. My hands trembled at the thought of it. Somehow, I finished dinner and brought it to the table. We sat and ate, them and me at the same table. It felt amazing to see them both actually enjoy what I had made. They loved it! I was deeply grateful for this moment.

They talked between themselves and I quietly ate, listening and being thankful that they couldn't read my thoughts. No man should feel this way so deeply, and yet I unquestionably did. It was who I am.

After they finished, I took their plates and poured them each more wine. I started to clean up the pans from cooking. Athena had a rule; I have to clean up the mess I made. No matter how much she enjoyed the meal, the mess was mine to clean up. This rule applied to more than dinner.

While I cleaned, they moved to a couple of chairs and continued to laugh and whisper. Sometimes, they were like little girls, giggling and speaking softly about things I'd never know. Occasionally, Athena glanced over and I saw that she was happy with me, happy with my progress as her property. Other times, I got the impression they were talking about me or perhaps some other man. Their laughter was too hearty and mischievous for it to be anything else.

The conversation turned to their favorite television show. Not surprisingly, they watched the same shows. Their mutual favorite was the mindless night-time soap opera, "Smash." I rolled my eyes. This escaped me! How such intelligent and powerful, not to mention incredibly alluring women could watch this crap, I didn't understand. Perhaps it was the mindlessness of it all, an escape from their day-to-day reality. I didn't know. They lit up when they discussed how much they hated this character, Karen, because "She's such a whiney bitch." Then a moment later, they were all giggly when they each hoped this guy, Derek, "Doesn't hook up with that girl, Ivy."

I tuned out. My own thoughts were too demanding, too intense and too much a part of my every waking moment to allow this kind of diversion. They almost had a life of their own in my head. There was no escaping this constant need to serve. Being in the home of Athena's friend, Bliss, made this need double in intensity.

I was so absorbed in my own thoughts, trying to wash the dishes, pots and pans without making too much noise, I didn't notice the conversation had changed. Perhaps it was the two bottles of wine they shared, or perhaps it was the closeness only women allowed each other in such a deep friendship. I didn't know. I did know that I was totally unaware that their wine glasses had been emptied, and that the mood of the room had changed. They were now whispering in each other's ear, maybe sharing something intensely personal. I hoped Athena was telling Bliss what I really was. I wasn't, as Bliss said, "a gentleman." Yes, I opened her door, no matter where we went. Yes, I carried her baggage, and pulled out her chair when she wanted to sit down. I took her coat as well, but it wasn't out of some archaic need to be a gentleman. I was her property. That is what she required of me, and for it she repaid me intensely, physically and carnally. I experienced a level of emotional and sexual fulfillment I've never had before. Athena didn't do anything falsely. She never let my needs outweigh her own. I was here because she wanted me to be. That was the single most amazing feeling I have ever felt.

Athena called to me from the couch they were sitting on, side-by-side, co-conspirators in the drama of their favorite mindless television show.

"Edge, our wine glasses are empty. Open another bottle, this time a Malbec, and fill them."

As I opened the bottle, I heard her say to Bliss quietly, "Yes I am serious. Do you really doubt it after all that you've seen?"

She was quiet. I looked over, recognizing the same expression I saw that first time under the desk in her office: an air of absolute confidence and surety. Athena knew what she was talking about without a doubt; the strength in her eyes made my legs tremble. It was about the sexiest thing I have ever seen, and she did it all the time.

Bliss replied, "No, I don't doubt it, but wow! Really?"

"Yes, I'll prove it."

I opened the bottle and walked to the couch, filling each of their glasses quietly. The tension in the room was undeniable.

Athena said, "Edge, when you're finished, put the bottle on the kitchen counter and come sit here, on the floor at my feet."

I did what she said and returned to the couch, sitting in front of them. Bliss sat up and crossed her legs. She put her glass down and gave us her full attention.

Athena said, "Edge, I want you to look at my friend here and tell her what you are."

I looked at Bliss and quietly said, "I am her property."

The room was silent.

Bliss then spoke, "And what does that entail, Edge?"

"I do whatever she asks, whenever she asks, exactly how she demands it."

"Wow! Really? No shit?"

I didn't answer. Athena swirled her wine in the crystal glass and looked at her friend.

"Yes!"

Bliss said, "Like what? What do you mean by 'whatever she asks?'"

Athena answered for me, "Whatever I ask, whenever I ask it, period."

"Like what?"

"Edge, be a good bitch, take off my pants, and carefully fold them on the floor next to me."

I unzipped her pants and Bliss said, "Holy shit, right here, now?"

I pulled her pants off her long legs and folded them carefully, laying them on the floor beside her. I faced her and Athena wrapped her legs around my shoulders.

She said, "Bitch, you'll do what we both know you were born to do. You'll make me come and while you do that, you'll look at my friend here. You'll not look away from her. Do you understand? I want her to see how badly you need to serve me."

I did what she asked, moving rhythmically up and down, licking and exploring her while Bliss watched me. It felt amazing to no longer hide from this woman who and what I was: property, a tool for Athena's pleasure. I pulled away from her and licked the cum off my lips. She had climaxed quickly, perhaps because her friend watching turned her on. Slowly, I teased her a little more, careful not to over stimulate her. She was always very sensitive after she came.

Bliss said. "Wow, you are serious!"

Athena turned to her friend and said, "You're next, if you would like."

Bliss was shocked. "Really?" She sat back and looked at us both. "I mean really?" Then Bliss said, "No, thank you, but no. I mean, it's been a long day and I haven't even showered."

Athena said, "Edge, does that matter to you?"

I replied, "No, it doesn't."

Bliss looked perplexed, interested, and yet unsure what she should do. Perhaps the wine had taken its toll on Athena and I. Maybe we were just too drunk to realize what we were saying. It looked like thoughts were spinning around her head.

Then I heard a voice, far away and distant, "Please! Let me serve you."

It was my voice speaking. I couldn't believe I had spoken that way. I had expressed to Athena how badly I was attracted to her friend, as long as I was doing as Athena required, but I had never asked any other woman to let me serve them before. Athena was surprised as well.

She added, "If you allow him to serve you, we have a couple of rules."

Bliss said, "What are they?"

"First, you must treat him like property. Do not be careful, and do not be gentle. He has one reason for being here, to do whatever you ask. Don't be concerned with what he wants, take what you desire and do it forcefully, without hesitation. If you can do that, he'll serve you."

"And the second rule?"

"You'll never call him by his name when he is between your legs. He's property, a thing, not a person. Call him 'bitch.' Be rough, grind against him hard, face fuck him as violent as you wish. There's nothing he won't do for you, but do not treat him with respect. Is that clear?"

"Yes! It's very clear."

They both stared at me quietly. I waited patiently; the ache in my chest was unbearable. God how I wanted this, dreamed about this.

Bliss spoke firmly, "Bitch, unbutton my pants."

I reached up, and one by one undid the brass buttons on her weathered and worn Levi 501s. I pulled her pants off and was pleasantly surprised that she wore no panties. One more thing the two women had in common: they always went commando.

Bliss had a glass of wine in her hand and said to me, "Bitch, take off your shirt. I want to feel your skin against my thighs while you suck and lick my clit."

I took off my shirt and spread her legs. She raised her hips and pushed firmly against my lips. At first, she wasn't wet but very quickly, she became a slippery mound, sliding and grinding against my mouth and tongue. I felt Athena's hand stroking my head while her friend rode me.

Athena said, "You're such an amazing little bitch. I was so lucky to find you!"

Bliss was very demanding and wanted me to lick her a specific way as she started to get into it. They both sipped her wine and glared at me, watching me as she ground her hips back and forth, up and down and then in small circles. It was always amazing how different women looked and tasted.

I pulled back and sucked her lips into my mouth, pulling them far from inside of her. Then I looked at both of them, ensuring they saw I had her lips in my mouth, gently holding them in my teeth. I pushed back onto her and made my lips hard, then rubbed them back and forth against her clit. This always made women crazy.

Bliss involuntarily raised her hips and spilled wine on her pussy. I devoured it as it flowed warmly between the folds. She laughed and purposefully poured more on her pussy. Again I responded and licked it all off.

She put the wine glass down and said, "Fuck this dancing around shit!"

Bliss took my head in both hands and began to forcefully grind her pussy against me, pumping faster and faster. She started to gasp and breathe heavily. I closed my eyes, only feeling the grinding wet pussy riding me rapidly. I couldn't think, I wanted this so badly and now it was here. Athena and Bliss were both using me, no blindfolds, no hiding. Bliss was nearly at climax and desperately, she demanded I lie on the floor. She straddled my face and rode me harder, grinding my head against the floor. Finally she came, screaming, her fingernails digging into my head and neck over and over.

She thrust against me gasping, angrily crying out, "Eat it, you fucking bitch!"

I did my best. When she came, it was a mouthful. Cum shot out of her, over and over. I willingly swallowed as much as I could. She was breathing heavily and turned around.

Bliss straddled me again and said, "Now lick my ass. Athena told me you love to lick ass. Show me!"

She rode me back and forth, and came again a few minutes later. She stayed on top, forcing my tongue deep in her ass, breathing heavily, and laughing. Finally, she dismounted and got dressed. My face was covered in her cum and sweat. I lay there for a few minutes, savoring this feeling of finally being complete.

I heard them both say, "Edge, you can get up now."

I stood, and they were both dressed and sitting back on the couch as if nothing had happened.

Athena said, "Our glasses are empty, Edge, and the dishes aren't done yet."

I stumbled out to the kitchen, to the wine bottle, and came back to fill their glasses. Then I finished the dishes. The two power women continued to talk and laugh as if nothing had happened, reinforcing the fact I was property, a thing to be used, and nothing more. It felt unbelievably good.

The next morning, we left. Bliss hugged us both goodbye and said, "I hope you'll come visit me again, I enjoyed it immensely."

Now that Bliss knew about me, I hoped Athena would allow them both to use me as often as they liked, as often as they wished. It was an amazing trip.

TEN

OUR HONEYMOON

It occurred to me re-reading the stories told here that I have shown a slanted view of the way things were. Monogamy in a relationship like ours is like using paper cups to drink a hundred dollar bottle of wine. It is meaningless, and spoils the whole point of ownership. She used me as she wished in whatever way she wished. Day in and day out was a constant display of the fact she owned me to everyone around us. Some thought it odd or curious. Others very much misunderstood, as I mentioned before, and thought I was a gentleman. Still others thought us promiscuous. We weren't. However, as you have read before, we were not sexually monogamous.

This point was driven home on our honeymoon in Jamaica. She purchased an all-inclusive package for seven nights and we were to be married there. I admit, I was surprised she wanted to marry to me a brief seven months after the day she forced me to make her come, while she pretended to work and talked to one of the men she was sleeping with at the time. She did, however, want to be married and made a point of spoiling me with this trip to the islands. It was a beautiful place, a Sandals resort with sandy white beaches and amazing food. The town was Ocho-Rios, you can look it up on the web, and we highly recommend it.

We arrived and got settled into our room. The balcony overlooked the city and resort. The view into the city was spotted with palms, and various other trees and flowers. It was very beautiful and very warm. We ate dinner and looked at the list of things to do. She planned out the week for us, asking what I would like to see or do while we were there and then making up an itinerary. We returned to our room and she showered then when it was my turn to shower, she got dressed and told me she'd be right back. I showered, and washed off the day's grime and sweat from travel. It felt good to be clean and refreshed.

When I came out of the shower, she still wasn't back so I got dressed and walked to balcony. I sat there for about an hour, looking out on the resort. The sun was going down and I was amazed at the view. The door opened behind me and I saw my future bride in the room, wearing an incredibly short form-fitting white dress, holding the hand of the man who had brought our luggage to the room. She had given him a pretty large tip and thanked him for his service. He was most grateful at the time. Athena later told me that she had found him attractive and decided to have a drink or two with him while I showered. They hit it off in the hotel bar and she invited him back to our room.

She loved his Jamaican accent and fit muscular body. He probably loved her short white cotton dress and incredibly long legs, which led up to her incredible ass. No doubt she had flashed her pussy to everyone in the bar, as she never wore underwear and sported the shortest dresses possible. The image of my future wife tormenting all the men and women in the bar with occasional glimpses of her freshly washed and smooth shaven pussy was intoxicating. My head swam. I shouldn't have been turned on by this, I should be furious. The constant conflict in my head was confusing.

She and the bellboy laughed as I entered the room from the balcony. She turned to face me and introduced us. His name was Ricky and I noticed he was nervous, unsure what to think. She had obviously picked him up for a reason, and we both eyed each other, wondering what she had in mind.

She said to me, "Edge, I want you to sit in that chair and do not move until I tell you to do so. Do you understand?"

I said, "Yes, I understand."

I knew from her tone and dark stare she meant it so I sat in the chair, putting my arms on the armrests, lightly gripping them.

She stared at me and said, "Can I get you a drink, Edge?"

"Yes, please."

She went to the mini bar and bent over in front of me and Ricky, showing off her long legs and completely naked ass and pussy while she pretended to struggle with finding a drink. It was obviously a very calculated move and apparently worked, as we were both mesmerized. After about thirty seconds of making sure we were both paying attention, she retrieved the drink and brought it to me.

She said, "Welcome to Jamaica, Edge. I hope you enjoy our honeymoon. I know I will."

Athena walked to Ricky and pulled him to the bed. She told him to sit there and as he did, he brought his hand up inside her thighs to her smooth pussy. Athena put one foot on the bed and opened her legs, allowing his rough calloused hands complete access to her. She pulled her dress up and closed her eyes, biting her lip while he explored her with his fingers. His exploration became more and more urgent, and she started to rotate her hips in small circles. Ricky looked at me, and I at him. Nothing was said between us, just an acknowledgement of each other's presence in the room.

He had his fingers deep inside my future wife while I sat in the chair, enjoying a cool drink, watching her gyrate and moan. The feeling was an incredible mixture of emotions. On one hand, I was totally engrossed in watching the scene unfold, trying to anticipate how the display of ownership she was about to make would affect me. On the other hand, I should have been disgusted. I would like to say I was, and angry as well. I wasn't. As wrong as it sounds, I was excited by the developing event. She knew exactly how to reach my darkest fantasies and make them reality.

Athena pulled the cotton dress over her head, and now she stood naked in front of him.

She said to me, as he pulled his hand away from her, licking the wet fingers one by one, "I told Ricky I'd pay him a hundred and fifty dollars to do whatever you instructed him to do to me. So, go ahead Edge, tell him what you want to see him do to me. It's my wedding gift to you. For this moment, you're in charge, but only for this moment. Make the most of it."

I wasn't sure what to say and had a hard time speaking. Clearing my throat, I thought it over. She had done this once before, given me brief control. It wasn't comfortable for either of us, this change of roles. I had failed miserably the last time and meant to make it up to her so this time,

I'd give her everything she wanted and more. That was what I failed to understand last time. I was still serving her, doing what she wanted, what she needed but I directed the scene. Ricky was her property and I'd be allowed to tell him how to please her. This way, she actually controlled us both. My job was to demonstrate I actually knew what she wanted, without her saying a word.

I knew her preferences, what she liked, really liked, and refused to go without. I told him to lie back on the bed. Then I told her to slowly remove all of his clothes. His cock was rock hard as he lay back, staring at my future wife's naked body.

She said, "Now what?"

"I want you to climb on the bed and suck his cock, but while you do it, you have to watch me."

She lay down on the bed and started to lick his balls. He was breathless with anticipation.

I said, "No, Athena, you can't lie on the bed. You have to keep your ass up, on your knees so I can see your pussy and your ass while you work his cock from top to bottom."

The sight of my future wife sucking another man's cock was strangely more erotic than I had ever imagined. She did it masterfully and had a lot of experience dominating men this way, leaving them emotionally and physically spent. Permanently, emotionally marked by her oral skills. No other woman would ever erase this memory for him. He didn't realize it but after this night, he'd never feel pleasure like this again.

She moaned as she took him deep into her throat, and came back off him over and over. I watched, fascinated as he grabbed the sheets, body rigid from the ecstasy. Athena took him to the edge of climax and then stopped. She always stopped to prolong the sex.

She licked the tip of his cock and said, "Mmmm, I like the taste of his cum." Smiling at me, she said, "Now what should I do?"

"Climb on top of him and face me. I want to watch him enter your pussy."

She mounted him and spread her legs wide so I could see everything. She slipped her hand down to guide his cock into her, and they both gasped as she firmly pressed down, forcing his cock deep inside her. Her mouth opened and she arched her back.

"Jesus, he's so deep inside me," she said.

Then she let out a deep animal-like moan. It was loud and uncontrolled. She ran her hands up her torso and rubbed her breasts hard, gritting her teeth.

"Edge," she gasped, "I love that you're watching him fuck me. Jesus, I own you! I've wanted you to watch this so badly."

She started to rock back and forth, riding his cock rhythmically and then in circles, one direction then the other. Finally, she ended it by coming completely off him and slamming hard down on his cock. She did this over and over. The physical violence of it, the animal need was breathtaking. Athena had never been this raw with me. I envied the guy and pitied him as well. This was a one-time shot; she would use his cock and then be done with him.

He mumbled some unintelligible words, incoherent words that meant nothing, being so entranced by her working him over. His brain couldn't function with this kind of domination.

Athena stopped slamming into him and rested on his hips, his engorged cock once again deep inside her. Smiling at me, she licked the fingers on her left hand, the same hand that wore the engagement ring I had given her. She reached down and started to rub her clit while she watched me.

She said, "I won't let him come inside me. He better not dare, however, I will come with his cock throbbing and filling me deeply." Then she exclaimed, "Oh God, Edge, I can feel his heart beating in his cock."

She closed her eyes and rubbed her clit faster and faster, moaning and breathing harder and harder until she came, pulling her fingers back while pressing hard on her clit, making it stand up, exposed and rigid.

She was breathing heavily and said, "Now what, my bitch?"

"Climb off him. Then get on your hands and knees on the bed."

She smiled, as she knew what that meant. I got out of the chair and took off my clothes, telling Ricky to stand in front of her while I went to the ass end of this fucking machine. I drove my cock into her brutally, just the way she liked it, over and over.

While I did this, I told him, "Face fuck the bitch! Make her suck you until she swallows every drop of your cum!"

We tag teamed her hard and relentlessly, thrusting in unison, the impacts on her body driving the other man's cock deeper into her. She made helpless animal sounds as we ravaged her. This may sound mean and brutal. In reality, she was totally in control the entire time. He was afraid he'd hurt her once, stopped, and pulled his throbbing cock out of her mouth.

"Are you all right?" he asked.

She was furious.

"Did I tell you to stop? Did I? You better earn that money, bellboy."

He was surprised and then went back to it, furiously pounding her, grabbing a hand full of her hair with each hand so she couldn't escape. Athena was gagging and moaning, but we both knew we had better not stop. He wouldn't escape until she was done with him. Finally, we both came: he in her mouth, and me in her pussy while she gulped and swallowed everything he shot into her mouth, or so I thought.

She pushed him away and said, "Very nice, Ricky! I'm glad you didn't disappoint me."

She made me get off of the bed, back in control now.

"Pay the man, Edge. Pay the man who just fucked your future wife."

Ricky was puzzled; he didn't expect to be treated like this. He didn't realize that he was just a toy, a cock to play with and she had finished with him. I paid him, and he quietly left, humiliated and confused. I turned back to her, after closing the door to the room and locking it. She stared at me.

She said, "Come here now, and tell me what you felt watching me fuck him."

I told her what I could, finding it hard to explain. I should be angry, hurt, and betrayed. Instead, I felt an intense sexual fascination seeing her with another man, watching her work his cock to her advantage, not caring at all what he felt, and surveying me the entire time. It was like watching her with a human dildo.

She said to me, "You really are an exceptional doormat, Edge. You really are!"

Most people would have been offended at this comment. I wasn't. She could wipe her feet or whatever else she wanted to on me any time she wished. I was her property.

Athena pulled me closer.

"Can you smell his cock on my breath, doormat?"

"Yes, I smell it."

She said, "Kiss me!"

It was not a request. She pulled me to her and kissed me, her tongue roughly entering my mouth, still covered with his cum. I thought she had swallowed it. She hadn't, not all of it. Angrily, she pushed me away, eyes burning in a dominant surge of feminine power and control.

"Now, you know my rule, my little bitch! Clean up the mess you made in my perfect pussy."

She forced my head between her legs to clean her cum-filled pussy, until she was satisfied she was spotless, watching me the entire time, complimenting my attention to the task. Later that night, after I had finished cleaning up the mess I had made, we lay in bed listening to the tropical evening sounds.

She said, "Thank you for knowing exactly what I needed, Edge. That was amazing."

I smiled, relieved I had pleased her. It was definitely a challenge. Welcome to our honeymoon.

ELEVEN

THE WEEK OF BLISS

I was busy cleaning the house again. After she received a phone call, she instructed me to prepare the house for a guest. I didn't know whom, it wasn't my place to ask, but they'd arrive tonight. It could be a man or woman. All I knew for sure was by the tone of her voice, Athena was excited this person would be visiting. I cleaned the guest bathroom until it shone and sparkled from every surface. Clean soapy smelling aromas filled the air and fresh, incredibly thick white towels hung from the towel bars. These were the guest towels, luxurious and soft. They were perfectly folded and the entire room was perfect. I changed the guest bedroom sheets as well, making the bed with the expensive nine hundred and fifty thread count sheets we only put on the bed for special occasions. For an added touch, I ironed the sheets until they were perfect and wrinkle free, sparing nothing in the preparations for this guest. It was my role as Athena's property to make the guest feel as welcome and appreciated as is humanly possible. This may sound ridiculous to others, but I found great satisfaction in making her proud of me, doing the extra little things she'd notice, knowing I have exceeded even her demanding expectations. Surprising her with excellence wasn't easy but definitely fulfilling.

I planned for dinner by making reservations at our favorite French restaurant. The food they prepare is unbelievably perfect. They match wines with the food flawlessly as well. It's a small intimate restaurant, with a warm ambiance. French music plays lightly in the background. The wait staff speak French and English, reading the French only menu to customers who couldn't understand it and they also make excellent recommendations. I wanted everything to be perfect for her guest. The French restaurant was the logical choice.

The house was clean and I had music playing throughout: Vivaldi. The piece was *The Four Seasons*, "Winter" to be specific. Everything was impeccable and I sat in front of the large glass window, waiting and watching for Athena and our visitor to arrive. She left a few hours ago to pick the mystery guest up from the airport and should be returning soon.

As dusk was just starting the gentle shift to darkness, Athena pulled up to the house and turned off the car's lights. I couldn't see who the guest was, I was a little apprehensive I admit. Athena likes it that way, keeping me on my toes, flexible to her needs. I sat quietly and tried to listen to their voices as they entered the house, walking up the stairway from the garage. I heard their footsteps, and the door to the basement opened. Athena must have asked our guest to be silent not to give anything away. She knows I am curious.

The door opened and I smiled, this was an amazing surprise indeed. The faces of two of the most interesting and amazing women I have ever met greeted me. Athena and her close friend, Bliss. We exchanged greetings and hugs, and I was embarrassed at how happy I was to see her. Now she said I may call her by her first name. This wasn't a request. It was stated as a request, but we all know now that deep in my soul, I was born to serve. I acknowledged the demand and smiled.

Athena said to me, "Edge, please grab Bliss' luggage from the car and take it to the guest room."

This was also not a request. I did so immediately. While I carried the three bags up the two flights of stairs to the guest bedroom, my head flooded with memories of the last time I saw the two women together. It was one of my most cherished memories and I became deeply engrossed in the details. Now it was obvious to me why she was so excited by the visit. Bliss had never been to the home we shared in Colorado. Athena took Bliss on a tour of the house while I put the suitcases in the guest bedroom. They laughed and talked as if no time had passed at all from our last visit. I was really glad I made the reservations for the French restaurant. The meal would be even more spectacular with the two women's enduring friendship and conversation.

We left for the restaurant a short time later and arrived a couple of minutes early for our reservations. I took Athena's coat and then asked Bliss if she would like me to take hers. The two women exchanged a glance that spoke volumes.

Bliss said, "Yes, Edge, I'd like that."

I took her coat and hung both of their coats up in the restaurant foyer.

The hostess came to us quietly and said, "Your table is ready. Please follow me."

The meal was exquisite; at least Athena and Bliss said so.

As we drank our wine, Athena said to me in a serious, meaningful tone, "Edge, while Bliss is here visiting us, you will serve us both equally, is that clear?"

This statement surprised me. I paused and said, "Equally?"

Never before had Athena made this statement. Did I hear her correctly?

She said, "Yes, as you would serve me, without question, without hesitation. Am I clear?"

I tried to say I understood, but my voice cracked and my mouth suddenly became dry. I took a drink of water, quickly putting the wine down, and cleared my throat.

"Yes," I said quietly, "I understand."

I couldn't look at either of them for a moment, being deep in thought. What had I done to deserve this unexpected and most definitely appreciated gift? It filled me with warmth as adrenaline flowed through my body. What an amazing day!

Athena raised her glass and made our traditional toast.

"Skoal," she said.

I picked up my glass of wine. All three of us repeated the toast, "Skoal," and clinked glassed. The two women stared at me, their eyes burning in the candlelight. I wish I could tell you I remember tasting the food; I don't. I do remember ordering the meal and eating it, but all I could think about was the look in their eyes as they toasted. Athena meant what she had said, and Bliss clearly intended to test my devotion to them both.

The meal passed in a blur of quietly listening to them catch up on the latest events of their lives. We finished and left the restaurant, full and contented. I think I was much happier at the gift they had given me than they were at being together, sharing their stories. We arrived home a short time later and said our good nights.

Athena said to Bliss, "I'll be leaving early, as I have appointments till the afternoon. What time would you like Edge to wake you up?"

Bliss looked at me and said, "Wake me at 8:00 a.m. I need to rest."

I agreed, and she went upstairs to her room. Athena and I got into bed in the master suite.

Athena asked me, "Are you holding up okay, Edge?"

"I'm fine."

"I'm expecting a lot from you this week. Bliss is my dearest closest friend. I want you to make every effort to make her visit an enjoyable one."

I nodded quietly and said, "I'll do as you ask."

"More importantly, Edge, I want you to do as Bliss asks, without hesitation. I cannot stress this enough. I know that you'll do your best."

She turned out the light and nestled her head onto my chest, falling asleep quickly. I didn't sleep for some time, as I lay there thinking about this unexpected turn of events.

TWELVE

THE NEXT MORNING

I must have finally fallen asleep, waking up the next morning to the alarm. It was six thirty in the morning. Athena turned it off and lay in bed a moment.

She ran her fingers through my hair and said, "Good morning, bitch, are you awake?"

I understood what she meant. She had a morning ritual. I woke her up every morning by licking her pussy, feeling her enthusiasm rise as she became more and more stimulated. This was how I started each day, providing her with pleasure from the first waking moment. Today, she wanted to watch me lick her pussy and lay facing me legs spread, smiling at my need to do this task at least once daily. Sometimes she lay on her stomach and had me lick her from behind. Either was fine as long as I pleased her, but I must confess, I preferred the more carnal, raw animal position of burying my face in her ass and licking her from behind.

Athena climaxed a few minutes later but continued to grind her pussy firmly against my face. I imagined her eyes burning as she controlled my every move and breath.

She said as she got out of bed, "Don't forget your appointment at 8:00 a.m. sharp, Edge."

She turned and smiled as she walked naked into the master bathroom, running the shower. An hour later, Athena had left for the day, and I was up, showered, shaved, and dressed. Five more minutes until I woke her guest.

I prepared a light breakfast of Greek yogurt mixed with berries and granola in a bowl with Bliss' favorite morning drink, a cup of green herbal tea. Walking up the stairs quietly and softly, I opened the door to the guest bedroom. The room was dark and I heard her soft breathing. I entered the room carefully, and placed the meal on the end table near the right hand side of the bed.

"Bliss, are you awake?"

No response. I lightly touched her shoulder, startling her.

"Good morning, Bliss."

She smiled and said, "Hi."

"How did you sleep?"

"Amazingly well. It's so quiet here."

"Yes, it is quiet, and peaceful."

I told her about the breakfast on the table next to the bed and she asked me to open the blinds to allow more light into the room.

I did as she asked and said, "Is there anything I can get you?"

"No, thanks, this is great. Has Athena left for the day?"

"She did about an hour ago."

She said, "So, just you and me for a while, huh?"

"Yes."

I was a little nervous at the mischievous smile on her face.

She smiled and said, "Uh huh."

I wasn't sure what this meant. It wasn't a statement, more one of those moments in which there was more in what was not being said than what was being said. Bliss had the comforter of the bed pulled up to her shoulders and hid under the blankets while she ate the meal.

She finished and said, "Thank you, bitch. That was perfect. Run me a bath. I like it hot, and add some bath salts. Let me know when it's ready, please."

She dismissed me just like that, and focused on the Blackberry smart phone she had laid out on the table near the empty dishes. I left the room and went down the hall to the guest bath, starting the water and waiting for it to reach the steaming temperature she had asked for. As the water filled, I added the bath salts she had requested, sprinkling them throughout the deepening water. Once the water had reached a comfortable depth, I walked back down the hallway to her room.

Bliss stood in front of the window. She had pulled the blinds up and was watching the garbage men as they pulled up to the can we kept at the base of the driveway. I was barely aware of the noise of the vehicle. She stood in the light, nude, watching the men dump the garbage. Reaching up, she stretched cat-like and limber. Her muscles rippled up and down her back as she reached up on tippy toes. Her body was quite different to Athena's, but no less perfect. Different but the same, intoxicating.

She turned and said, "Is the tub ready?"

"Yes."

Bliss smiled playfully, fully aware I had been admiring her silhouette in the window. She walked past me down the hallway and entered the bathroom. Bliss had runners' legs; she took part in marathons for "fun" and I fully appreciated the impact the training had on her body. Athena was more curvy and soft, but both women were sensual in their own way.

I went to the window and noticed the garbage man had also been watching her. He saw me, smiled, and waved. I shrugged and smiled back. Today would be day one of the entire week of her visit. So far, it had been nothing too challenging but in the back of my mind, I remembered Athena's statement that she wanted me to make her guest as comfortable as possible and fulfill her every request. I had butterflies in my stomach thinking about it.

Walking back to the bathroom, I stood outside the door and asked if she needed anything else.

Bliss responded from inside the bathroom, "Come in please, I have a question."

I walked into the steam filled room and looked at her lying in the tub.

She said, "The tub feels amazing. Can you reach the washcloth for me?"

I did so and brought it to her.

"Take the soap and make a substantial lather with it, please." Again I did this. "Yes, very nice. Now wash me."

Bliss leaned forward and I carefully washed her face. She closed her eyes while I did this and then rinsed off in the fragrant water. As she handed me her arm, I washed it, then her foot and her calf came out of the water, I washed them both as well. I went in a counter clockwise direction around the tub as she lifted each arm and leg for me to wash. Finally, she slowly got up and turned around facing away from me. I washed her shoulders first and worked my way to the small of her back, stopping for a moment as I remembered Athena's words. I washed her ass and slipped the washcloth in her muscular cheeks, carefully cleaning her, and then worked my way down her thighs. Looking up, I saw Bliss watching me with a slight smile on her face.

I said, "Would you like to turn around?"

"Yes, I would." She turned around as she added, "Work your way back up now."

I washed the front of her thighs and worked my way up. Just as I reached the top of her thighs, she took one leg out of the water and put it on the edge of the tub, opening up her legs and pussy for me to wash.

"Continue."

I carefully cleaned her, warming the washcloth in the hot bath water. Bliss said nothing but she watched my every move. I washed her firm abdomen and cleaned each of her small but firm breasts. She raised her arms and I washed under them as well.

When I finished she said, "Well done."

She sat back down into the hot water and rinsed off, looking around the tub. A dark look came over her face.

"Bitch, you forgot something. What do you see that's missing, that should be here?"

I was at a loss. I said, "I don't know. I'm sorry, I don't know what I've missed."

She said quietly, disappointed, "A razor and baby oil, bitch. I need to shave my legs."

I was already failing.

"Yes, you're right. I'll be right back."

I went to the master bathroom and returned with them.

She didn't look at me for a moment but then said, "This blade isn't new, bitch, it's been used."

My face flushed. "I am sorry."

I quickly left the room and returned with a new blade, replacing the old one and handing the razor back to her.

She said, "Oh no, you will shave me."

The idea terrified me. I had failed already, and if I accidentally nicked her skin, this day would be irretrievably ruined.

I said, "Perhaps—"

She stopped me mid-sentence, "Yes, *bitch*? Perhaps what?"

I said nothing at all. Her disappointment was obvious.

"Perhaps I should apply the baby oil, before I start shaving."

She stared at me for a brief moment and said, "That's what I expected."

I nodded and began to pour the oil over her left leg, rubbing it in and then I started to shave her legs. I worked my way up to the knees and felt the area I had shaved.

"You've done this before I see," she said.

I had. Athena had me shave her body when the whim arose. She hates body hair and has very little except for a thin "landing strip" of pubic hair. It was my task to keep it perfectly trimmed and attractive.

I replied, "Yes, I have."

Bliss said, "I know. Athena told me of your attention to detail. I'm excited to see how well you can do this. Tell me, bitch, do you remember the night you showed me how you need to be owned by powerful women?"

I said I did. The memory was intensely and permanently burned into my mind.

"I remember it as well, bitch. After you've finished shaving me, I'd like to explore that further."

I'd be most grateful to explore that with Bliss.

"First, however, you'll need to finish this task."

I rinsed the razor and carefully shaved the area around the public bone. Bliss preferred her pussy completely shaved and smooth. I finished what I could reach and she turned around, spreading her legs in the tub. One foot was now at each end of the tub.

She said, "I want to be completely smooth. Start where you would lick me if I required it and make sure you miss nothing."

I took some time not to exclude any small hairs hidden in the folds of skin. I ran my fingers up and down, exploring her and searching for hair I may have missed. Finally, I was satisfied that she was perfectly smooth.

She stood up and said, "Nicely done. Let the water out now." I released the water. "Now we need to wash my hair."

We washed her hair after I refilled the tub, rinsing off the sides. Bliss has long black hair with some curl. Finally, it was washed, rinsed, conditioned, and rinsed again. She asked me to grab a towel and dry her off. I did so, and she walked to her room and dressed for the day.

THIRTEEN
AFTERNOON

We spent the first half of the day just hanging out in the house. It was comfortable and relaxed. I combed her hair while she read a magazine. No, she didn't read *People* or *Us Weekly*, she read *Foreign Affairs*. She wasn't your average woman by any means.

About one in the afternoon, her cell phone rang and she answered it. It was her current man, Mr. Right Now, not Mr. Right. She smiled as they talked, and settled back into one of the two over-stuffed leather chairs in the living room. They indulged in small talk and then finally, I saw the conversation had become more intimate. She made small "uh huh" sounds and then, "Yes, I'd like that." I pretended not to listen.

As I worked on my latest book, I heard a couple of finger snaps so I looked over to discover she was holding her glass up. She wanted more to drink. I got up, refilled it and brought it back to her. Bliss took the glass and placed it on the end table, next to the over-stuffed chair. She pointed at me, motioning for me to drop to the floor in front of her. I paused. She motioned again more angrily for me to get on the floor. I did so and she lay back in the chair, legs slightly spread in front of her.

She said clearly to the voice on the phone, "I'm taking off my pants now. Tell me what you would do to me."

Bliss motioned with her head to remove her pants. I did so. She was wet, and the appearance of her shaved and perfect pussy was breath taking.

She said, "Yes, I'm touching myself."

Spreading her legs wide, she held up her hand to indicate I finger her while she talked to him. I did as she asked. Each time she told him what she was doing, I mirrored her comments.

"Tell me what you would do now. If you were here, I'd have you lick my ass."

Bliss pulled her legs up and wider, and I did as she described, pressing my tongue inside her and then dancing around the sensitive areas of her ass.

"Yes!"

I could almost feel it now as I deeply explored her spread cheeks.

"Oh yes, I really want to come but it's so hard to imagine what you feel like inside me. Talk to me baby; tell me about your cock inside me."

I stopped cold. I have never had sex with another woman since I met Athena. I didn't know what do to. Bliss motioned for me to lie on the thick black floor rug on which I knelt. I hesitated, not knowing what to do. Bliss covered the phone so that he couldn't hear her speak.

"What did Athena tell you, bitch?"

I remembered what I'd been told and removed my pants. I was hard and throbbed with each heartbeat. She smiled and mouthed the words, "I like that a lot."

She said to the man on the phone, "Yes, I can imagine you lying in your bed now... Uh huh, I take you in my mouth to tease you."

Bliss did that to me and I involuntarily arched my back as the sensations flooded my body. I gasped as she expertly sucked my cock.

She said, "Yes, now I want to ride you! Tell me how hard you are."

Her man responded as she guided me inside her. Once I started to enter her, she sat down forcefully and cried out.

She said, "Yes baby, I can almost feel it throbbing inside me."

I heard his excited voice on the phone saying, "Fuck me, baby fuck me hard."

She did just that and rode me, her hips thrusting rapidly back and forth, not even aware of my reaction. I was meat between her legs, nothing more. Once again, this wasn't her having sex with me, this was ownership. She owned me and used me. I understood now and the fear left me. I was to please her regardless of what she wanted so I did my best to make the most out of her riding me.

"I want you to take me from behind now, baby." She climbed off me, on her hands and knees in front of me now. She said into the phone, "Take me from behind, and fuck me hard."

I did as she told her man to do.

Several minutes later she said, "Tell me how you would lick me."

His voice was rapid on the phone, excited by her enthusiasm for this alleged phone sex. I licked her ass and pussy deeply, and she cried out.

"Seriously, I swear I can feel your tongue inside me."

I thought to myself, *Yes you can!*

I made the most out of this display of ownership as I could.

Finally she said, "Ok, now I want to finish back on top of you. Tell me how you're lying back down on the bed."

I lay down on the floor and she slid me back inside her. Bliss began to work me back and forth and then in circles, over and over talking to her man on the phone and fucking me. Her nails dug deep into my chest and her thrusts become more frantic.

"I'm so close, oh God, I'm close."

She looked into my eyes and I saw she needed this badly. The animal need was incredible. I grabbed her hips with both hands and she told him, "Put your hands on my hips and grind me."

He said something I couldn't make out. I thrust upward, driving my cock deep inside her and at the same time, I took control of her hips, hammering them back and forth, hard and fast. Her breathing was frantic now and finally she said, "Oh God, yes, here it comes!"

I no longer felt her nails, or heard her voice. I came as well and felt the cum shooting inside her. A few moments later, she was breathing more regularly and started to talk to him again.

"Baby, I've always wanted you to lick me off after you fuck me. Would you do that?" She listened and then said, "Why not?"

He said, "I won't do that for you."

She said, "That's ok, baby." She lifted herself off my cock and mounted my face. "Let's pretend that you'd do it."

A few moments later, I was covered in both of our cum. She rode my face and talked to him about her "imagined" fantasy. She came again, climbed off me and sat back in the chair. Legs spread, she motioned for me to continue cleaning up the cum that had been spread around her pussy and ass from the face fucking I just received. I did as she asked until her call was finished. Bliss watched me intently while speaking to her man about how she missed him. Finally, she hung up.

She pulled my head away from her and stared at me. She said nothing for several minutes, looking deep into my eyes.

Finally she said, "My, you really do need this don't you, bitch?"

I nodded.

Bliss told me, "I'm most satisfied at your attention to the task. How does that make you feel? Do you feel loved?"

"No, I feel used, and it's more amazing than I could ever explain."

"That's good, bitch. You are a good little bitch, aren't you? I'm glad you don't feel loved, Edge, because that would be confusing. I don't love you but I do enjoy how much I can use you. Now go wash that cum off of your face and brush your teeth, you smell like ass."

She smiled, and went to her bathroom upstairs while I went to shower.

FOURTEEN

LATER THAT DAY

A thena came home later and asked Bliss about her day. She said she'd had an excellent day and that her boyfriend had called. I made dinner for them and later, after drinking an excellent Zinfandel wine, we went to bed. Athena asked me about the day and I told her every detail. She was noticeably disappointed when I mentioned forgetting the razor and baby oil. However, when I detailed the story of Bliss and her conversation on the phone to her man, Athena smiled.

She kissed me and said, "Thank you for not disappointing me, or my friend. I love how I can count on you to completely submit to any request she or I make."

There was no jealousy, no fear. Athena knew I belonged to her unequivocally.

"Edge, I had a very long day, busy and stressful. I need you to make me forget that."

She climbed on top of me and sat on my face, grinding her ass on my tongue and mouth. While she faced away from me, she made me lick her ass and pussy until she had come repeatedly and loudly. Occasionally, she lay down and bit my hard cock, just hard enough to hurt, but not hard enough to break the skin. Athena did this over and over, punishing me for forgetting the razor. It hurt and felt amazing at the same time. I fell into a deep sleep after she'd finished using me, the sweaty scent of her unwashed ass and pussy still on me.

The rest of the week passed like this. I bathed them both, and shaved them both. I painted their toenails while they talked in our living room. I prepared every meal they ate. They poured wine on their pussies while they sat on the benches on our front porch. I licked it off while they talked and watched the sun set. I licked their asses whenever they demanded, and tasted my own cum over and over, day after day. Athena had a rule, and Bliss apparently liked the rule as well; I clean up the mess I make. I did my absolute best to be an exceptional doormat. Most men would cringe at the thought of being owned by two women like this. To me, it was a final affirmation of what I have always known about myself and kept deeply buried. I was born to serve, to be used. It wasn't sex. It wasn't love. It was power and control. I didn't know what I did to deserve such a gift, but I was extremely grateful.

A week after Bliss had left and returned to her new assignment at a prestigious military academy, Athena and I sat on the front porch again, watching the sunset.

"Edge, you've been really quiet since Bliss left. You look deep in thought."

"I am."

Athena said, "I'm listening."

"I think it's too bad that we all can't live in one house. I could serve you both. They say a man cannot serve two masters. I know I could serve both of you extremely well, without hesitation."

Athena smiled and said, "I agree, it would be nice for me as well. Bliss and I get along very well. We're like kindred spirits. We've traveled all over the world together, and it's the most comfortable I have been with anyone." Athena paused for a moment and said, "You never know what can happen. I guess we'll see."

FIFTEEN

THE WINE CLUB

Athena had a remarkable collection of wines from all over the world. It wasn't as impossible as it sounded to be able to collect them. She belonged to a wine club online and ordered the best the club had to offer. We received a case or so every two to three weeks, and I placed them in the two dual-zone wine fridges that we had in the dining room. The wines were grouped by type and then country of origin. Every night after dinner, she asked me to open a wine that she picked out and pour it for us.

We sat in our living room and looked out at the sunset. The view was spectacular. There were five separate mountain ranges you could see from the large bay window that looked out over our land. Every day wasn't a display of her domination over me. Some days, she just wanted to be together...drink wine, talk, laugh, and share dreams. I admit, I wasn't always comfortable sharing my dreams. My dreams were dark, at least to me, and the need to be owned was nearly as strong as the need to survive, to breathe, and maybe if I am truly honest, stronger than that.

She sometimes apologized for not constantly dominating me on every occasion, and I realized she did care about my needs. I just didn't want to hear that she loved me. I didn't want to be loved, *owned,* yes. Love was a façade to me. I had no need to be loved. Reading back through the ac- counts of our life, I realize that you may think it was one constant face fuck. Periods of time went by where Athena didn't dominate me as deeply as I needed or would have liked. Some days, she forced me to submit to nothing more than pouring wine and watching the sunset. Other days, she required me to sit on the couch and only allowed me to caress her naked body while she spread her legs in front of me. With a dark and knowing smile, she dominated me by doing nothing more than lying naked while she flaunted herself. She tormented me in this way and many others.

Athena had a very intriguing habit when she first started to include me while she drank wine. She took a mouthful of wine into her mouth and kissed me. While she kissed me, she released the wine into my mouth and told me to swallow it. It was very erotic and sensual, and I have no idea why. To feel the wine shooting into my mouth, coming from her body, her mouth, was an indescribable feeling. The taste of the wine mixed with her flavors was intoxicating. Her eyes were just as intoxicating while she stared at me, watching my reaction as she forced me to take it in and swallow. She didn't tell me what she was thinking. I didn't really need to know, but I did need to see that look in her eyes. I needed to feel the passion and maybe the insanity of this ownership we both cherished so deeply.

Our life was much like the wine we drank. Different wines pair well with different foods and spices. Some people we knew only liked white wines and couldn't understand our passion for the more bold and complex reds. Reds have depth the white wines cannot match. If you are a wine drinker, you will understand this analogy. Whites are crisp and nice no doubt, and leave you with the desired effect. They pair well with most meals as well. Reds, however, complement the dark side of the menu, red meat, spices, pepper, and flavors that make you taste things you may not have known existed.

We sought the bolder reds: Zinfandels, Malbecs, Cabs, and Pinot Noirs that make you stop and take notice. We had over three hundred bottles of these red wines in our fridge. They awaken your pallet with four or five intense flavors, experiencing one after another in each swallow. If you can understand this, then you can understand our insane need to be in this relationship. She owned me, shared me with whomever she chose. I served her and when I was truly fortunate, she allowed me to serve others.

We were not traditionally monogamous. We were, however, unconditionally in this. There was no doubt of the commitment by either of us. It was beyond the standard relationship, just as the red wines we drank were more complex and deep than the white wines most people in the world favored. You cannot comprehend the depth here if you favor the "white wine lifestyle." Believe me, there's nothing like tasting one of these bold complex reds, as Athena or the power woman she shared me with poured it over their pussy while I licked it off. Our lifestyle and our wines were very much a part of the way we saw life. We lived with complexity and needed to explore the tastes and flavors that are out there.

I was working on creating a man-made stream on our land. Athena decided she wanted to have more wildlife and after we both talked it over, she concluded that more running water on our land would draw in the wildlife present in the area. The path of the stream was divided into two separate starting points that eventually joined and flowed over a waterfall into the reservoir at the end of the stream. There, the water was collected and pumped back up to the top, where it started over again. It was a big project. The soil was rocky, and contained large boulders in the path she had decided the stream would take. I had been working on the streambed for weeks, removing the huge rocks by hand and carving out the path in the mountainside. The combined path of the two streams would be two hundred feet in total.

The labor helped me focus my mind while Athena was out of town. She left on a business trip, and usually found some way to remind me that she owned me while absent. She sent me text messages telling me what she was doing, and with whom. Sometimes, it was just work, other times it wasn't. She described sexual trysts to me she'd had with people she worked with, telling me about their different sexual fantasies, things she did with them, or things they did to her. I received pictures of naked men tied to some hotel bed, their faces covered in her cum.

Previously, she had me take pictures of her naked and then made me send them to her other male partners. She told them it was me that took the photos, and asked them and me how it felt to know the other man knew about you. It was a strange set of emotions, knowing that she hid nothing from me. If this was a white wine relationship, I'd be enraged. It wasn't, however. This was a bold flavored, red wine relationship, so I wasn't angry. She hid nothing from me. There were no lies between us. She had me unconditionally serve her women friends while she watched and displayed her control over me in many ways. This was just another display, another way she fulfilled my darkest, most deeply guarded need to be owned and used. Athena did it expertly.

SIXTEEN

BATHTUB PREP

The phone buzzed in my pocket, and I stopped hammering away at the streambed with the pickaxe. I was tired and covered in sweat. I pulled the phone from my pants pocket and looked. It was a message from her, a picture text again. The last picture she sent had been taken by her. It was a short clip with sound. Athena was going down on some guy she had met and had him completely submitting to her will. She took the GIF as he came in her mouth, and she opened up to show me the cum. Then she forced him to kiss her and forced it back into his mouth like she had done with the wine to me on so many occasions. He was her property as well, but only for a short while. Soon, she'd kick him to the curb, and he'd be left to look for another woman to fill the vacant empty hole in his soul.

Today, the GIF was of Athena and another woman at a club, smiling and waving.

Athena said, "Say hi to my property, Edge."

The woman said, "Hi Edge, hope to meet you soon."

The GIF restarted, over and over until I ended it. I guessed she was bringing this woman home with her. Then the phone buzzed again. The text said she was bringing her new friend to the house tomorrow, "Please have the house ready and dinner for two. She will be staying the night. Thanks Edge, see you then, Athena."

The message told me volumes of what would be expected. I'd select a dinner and prepare it for Athena and her guest. I wouldn't be dining with them, I'd be serving them and attending to their every need. This would be a display of her ownership of me. I decided on a fairly meat-heavy dinner of filet mignon and pheasant, with a side of various vegetables. I would pair this meal with a Malbec that we just received from the wine club. It was a bottle of Broquel Malbec 2009; Broquel means "shield" in Argentina. The wine would be excellent with the two meats, an excellent addition to the mixture of flavors.

Finally, all the preparations were made, and the sheets on Athena's bed had been washed and ironed. The house was clean and a light scent of jasmine permeated the air. I had prepared the upstairs rooms for our guest. Athena sent me a text telling me they were on their way and I started the meal, as they'd be here in an hour or less.

I heard the sleek sports car that Athena drove coming up the two-mile long driveway to our home. The car was Italian, a 1986 Bertone X-19, a two seat, hard top convertible. It was red over grey and in immaculate condition. She pulled into the garage and I listened to the garage door close as I made the final preparations for dinner.

The two women came upstairs from the garage and the doorway opened. A strikingly beautiful woman stood with Athena. She had short, closely cropped hair and deep dark eyes, I couldn't make out if she was of Hispanic or Asian descent. She was tall like Athena and athletically built. She looked at me but made no visual connection at all, gazing through me as if I didn't exist. She didn't smile or even acknowledge my presence.

Athena didn't introduce us. She simply asked, "When will dinner be ready?"

I replied, "In five minutes."

"That's perfect as usual, Edge. Thank you."

She took the woman on a tour of our home and I brought the food to the table as they finished, pouring the wine for each of them and making sure they had everything they needed.

"That'll be all, Edge. Thank you. I'll call if we need anything else."

I went to the guest room upstairs and relaxed, looking out the window, listening to the muffled sounds of their conversation one floor below. They talked and laughed as if they had known each other for years. I heard their glasses click as they toasted their new friendship and it sounded like they were kissing. Athena called to me and I came downstairs.

"I'd like you to run a bath for us in the master bathroom. Add bath salts and bubbles but before you do, open another bottle of wine for us."

I did as she asked, pouring the wine in each glass and then leaving the rest on the table for them. Moving to the master bath, I started the water in the large Jacuzzi tub that was built into the floor, making the preparations as she had asked, adding the bath salts and bubbles at the last minute. The bath was ready and I returned to the dining area.

Athena got up and took her friend's hand. They grabbed their glasses of wine and Athena led her to the master bath, putting her wine down on the edge of the tub. She then took the woman's wine glass and did the same with it, caressing the woman's face and kissing her ardently. They responded to each other, kissing and petting while I stood silently nearby.

When they stopped, Athena told me to remove their clothing. I did so carefully and folded each garment after it had been removed, placing it on the countertop near the sink. The women silently watched each other and me until they were completely naked. Then I assisted them as they descended into the bathtub's steaming and fragrant water. Athena asked me to stand by quietly while they bathed and drank wine, in case they needed something. I did so, a manservant of the two women, Athena's property. They frequently kissed and reached for each other under the thick cover of bubbles, touching and exploring while they passionately kissed. They took turns each exploring the other, giving in to the other.

Finally, Athena said to me, "You'll be shaving each of us. Make sure you have a fresh razor."

I did so, wondering where this night would take the three of us. I carefully shaved each of them while the other watched. There was nothing sexual about this, it was a task the manservant had been asked to complete, nothing more. They inspected my work, hands sliding up and down each other's now smooth legs, ass and pussy.

Once they were satisfied the shaving was perfect, Athena said to me, "We'll be getting out now, bring us towels."

I brought them and carefully wrapped each of them in a towel. As they enclosed themselves in the luxurious cotton, Athena told me to get the nail polish and make preparations to paint each of their nails. The women walked out to the living room and dropped the towels on the floor. I sat on the floor, and began to paint each toenail while the two women watched me silently. They taunted me by spreading their legs as I tried to concentrate. I hadn't been instructed to do anything else but paint their nails. They tormented me with this display of sexuality and dominance. Finally, I finished.

Athena said to me, "You'll be staying in the guest bedroom tonight. Is my bed properly prepared?"

I was surprised at this but said, "Yes, it's ready."

"That'll be all then."

I went back upstairs and sat in the rocking chair in front of the window. A few minutes went by, and I heard them moaning and an occasional gasp of ecstasy as each pleasured the other. I finally fell asleep in the guest bed after Athena climaxed loudly and then giggled.

The next day, I awoke at 6:00 a.m. and prepared Athena's usual breakfast. I quietly entered the room and woke her up. She and the woman were still naked and entwined in a lover's embrace of sleep and comfort. They woke up and I asked the woman what she would like for breakfast.

She said, "Just coffee, black please."

I left and prepared the coffee. The women got up, showered, and prepared for the day. At noon, Athena told me to drive her friend to the airport to catch a flight. This was a short visit. Usually, her guests stayed longer and I was required to do more than run a bath and pour wine. However, I was her property, I did as I was told and took the woman to the airport.

During the journey, she made no attempt to make small talk. She wasn't interested in men at all, least of all the property of the woman she had spent the night with. I carried her bags into the airport. She said that will be all, turned and walked away. I didn't know where she was from or where she was going. I didn't even know her name.

After returning home, I did the normal tasks I complete after Athena has a friend stay. Some guests were men, some were women like last night. The tasks were always the same. I washed the bedding again, cleaned the tub, washed the dishes, and once everything was clean, I put the entire house back the way it was.

Later that night, Athena had me sitting on the couch again. A fire burned in the fireplace and the house was cozy and warm. The lights were off and the fire warmed the house with its soft light. She was nude and I caressed her skin, lightly touching her, still smooth and soft from being shaved the previous night. Athena told me about her night, and the sex she shared with the dark haired woman while I sat silently listening, feeling owned again, although this time it was emotionally owned. No sexual ownership of me had occurred for days. The quiet, athletic woman she brought to the house satisfied Athena's needs. She did this to remind me of her power over me. I could touch her but nothing more; I would suffer while I waited for her to sexually dominate me again. It could be several days.

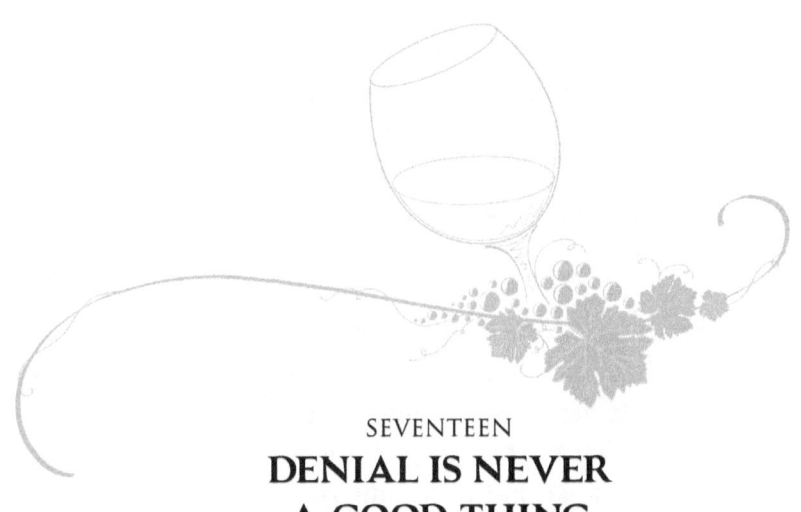

SEVENTEEN

DENIAL IS NEVER
A GOOD THING

What I thought would be several days turned into three weeks, three weeks of not being dominated to the depth or darkness I desperately needed. The pain was unbelievable. To those of you who drink "white wine" and are satisfied by it, maybe being in pain seems unreasonable or perhaps exaggerated. I really wish I didn't know this reality.

Before I met Athena, I denied this need. I was mean and vicious, and would do anything to try to make this constant ache go away. I had meaningless sex with any mean and vicious woman I could find, trying to meet this need. Although I knew what I was looking for, finding it seemed impossible. I went into clubs when I worked in the Vice Unit and watched the women, looking for that certain air. I'd recognize it when I saw it. Reality was, I never found it. It was the equivalent of going to the pet store and hoping to find a wolf, searching the store day after day until finally, you realize the only thing they carry are toy cup poodles, tiny harmless frail poodles. I needed a wolf and needed her badly.

My wolf had been very different since the woman who looked through me had stayed the night. I didn't know what she was trying to teach me and if I should ask. Finally one day, she drove me out of my comfort zone with the constant flaunting of her body, which she was barely covert about and she bent over in front of me, a silent invitation to take her. The confusing denial of any overt domination combined by this suggestive flirting drove me insane.

Eventually, one night I got a call from her when she was on the way home from work. Athena told me to be showered, shaved and waiting for her at the top of the stairs. She sounded angry. I was waiting at the top of the stairs when she came home. She glared at me as she came up the stairs, pushing past me and dropping her bags on the table.

"Bitch," she said, "I've just about had it with this whiny fuck you've become."

She grabbed me by the throat and pushed me against the wall.

She scowled at me and said, "That beautiful woman who was here had me thinking. I told her about you and she said you were just like every other man I have known. You're using me! You're using me in a different way than they did, but still using me just the same. I won't be used by any man ever again." She spun me around and said, "Put your hands behind your back, bitch."

I did so and she bound them with what felt like wire. It was tight and hurt.

She said, "Good, now get down on your knees."

She shoved me roughly to the hardwood floor and I fell over.

"Fuck! Look at you, my little bitch can't even stand up straight."

Athena grabbed me by the hair and coarsely pulled me to an upright position. She then quickly tore off her business suit and stood in front of me.

"I see the need in you to serve me, bitch. You desperately want to please me, don't you?"

I said, "Yes, I do."

She turned around and said to me, "Lick my nasty ass then, my little bitch boy."

Athena rode me hard, sliding her ass up and down while I tried to lick her. It was what I needed but it was humiliating. They say you should be careful what you wish for, and I had wished for this for three weeks. She rode me until she felt satisfied.

Then she turned around and said to me, "You make me sick! Most men would want to fuck my brains out, but all you can think of is licking my ass and cunt day in and day out. Stand up, pussy!"

She removed the wire from my wrists, and then walked into the bedroom. She lay down on the bed and said, "Bring me my phone. I'm going to call someone with a cock who knows what to do with it."

I was getting angry. I was her sub definitely, exceptional doormat, you bet! But this was disrespect, not domination. She rolled over, and stuck her naked ass in the air as she came up on her knees and faced away from me.

"I can't wait to feel a cock inside me, it's been too long…. Do you have my phone yet, bitch? You can even stay and listen if you like, while I dream about this other man fucking me."

I snapped. I admit I lost it. The sight of her spread legs and perfect ass up in the air for the taking was too much. I took off my pants and launched myself on top of her. Grabbing both hands and pinning them behind her back with one hand, I seized a fist full of her hair with the other. I pulled her head up and told her to get up on her knees. She was furious and fought me, but I was no longer sane. I was enraged at the denial she had put me through, and now she was going to another man? Maybe, but not until she felt my rage and my cock inside her.

I hurt her enough so that she finally got up on both knees, placing her wet cunt in striking distance. I drove my cock deep into her, brutally.

"How's that, you arrogant fucking bitch? I should have done this to you that very first day in your fucking office."

I pounded her over and over, relentlessly driving my painfully hard cock into her and pulling her hair viciously. I'd had it with this bullshit. The pain was too intense, I couldn't take this anymore. Even a sub has their limits and I had reached mine. When she finally fell silent and no longer fought me, I pushed her face into the bed, still pounding relentlessly. I couldn't come no matter how hard I tried. Finally, I released her, rolling her over on her back. I pushed her legs up onto my shoulders.

Grabbing her hair again with both hands, I pulled her head back and said, "How does it feel to be owned, you fucking bitch? I hate you for what you have denied me."

Athena glared at me, breathing deep and panting while I slammed inside her, over and over. She watched me, never taking her eyes off me, watching the violent thrusts of my hips and the rage and desire in my eyes. Finally I came. Grabbing her hair, I pulled her close and said, with every hard and spasmodic thrust, "Take it you fucking bitch, take every fucking drop."

I knew that she was through with me now. There was no way she could ever forgive such a transgression of who we were. I had been driven insane by pain, lust, and had lashed out at her. She could never forgive this.

I rolled over and thought to myself, *My life is over. She'll leave me now.*

Sitting there, I regretted what I had done. A little girl-like giggle came from her and I opened my eyes. She was looking at me and smiling.

"Finally you admit, you are a sub, but you have your limits. It's good to know there is still a feral animal in you, the feral animal I saw in you that first time I caught you trying to get a look up my skirt. I could tell you needed more than most women understood. I could tell you needed to be owned. I didn't know if you still had this animal side in you until now. I thought maybe I'd broken you forever. Look at me, my sub."

I did, ashamed of what I had done.

Athena said, "As much as you need to be owned and dominated, I need to dominate you. We're like Yin and Yang, do you understand?"

I did, I have never known such balance in my life. Until lately, this had been perfect.

She said, "But even in the Yin and Yang symbol, there's a part that's the opposite, the black side has a small white circle, the white side has a small black circle. It's all about balance. Occasionally, my perfect bitch, you'll have to remind me that you're still a man. You may be my bitch, but you're still a man, do you understand?"

I thought I did. Athena needed to be reminded that even though she dominated me day after day, I could still be drawn to her in an animalistic carnal way, that the rules could be broken, and I would take her. She needed that like I needed to be dominated. We were still subject to the same basic animal instincts in spite of our emotional needs. This created an emotional conflict, but I have to admit, I was tired of waiting for her. She was right, there had to be balance.

I said, "What the hell did that woman say to you to make you think I was broken?"

"She told me that no man would ever be so devoted to any woman as you appeared to be to me. She said the only way to tell if you were truly being honest was to drive you to the point you couldn't take it anymore.

If you snapped, went crazy and carnal on me, then you were truly serving my needs first, subordinating to me even though it caused you pain. I see now that you've been in extreme pain and that I truly do own you. As deep and as dark as your soul is, I own it all. But what you have to realize as well, you own me. You make my balance possible as well. We fit, dark and light, sub and Domme. Now get over here and clean up this mess you made, my little bitch."

I said, "Fuck that, I'm not doing it."

I was still in pain and pulling away from her. Once the rage had started to resurface, it was hard to contain. The old me came back, mean, nasty and defiant.

She said, "Yes you will."

Athena climbed on top of me and rode my face hard, forcing me to clean her off. Finally, my pain was gone. I suppose hers was as well. We were back where we each belonged, without doubts.

There was a part of me that strongly wanted to be irrevocably owned and possessed by Athena. Obviously, as you have read, she took whatever she wanted, whenever she wanted it and I'd do whatever I could to serve her. There was a part of my need that may seem really bizarre to someone outside of this. Typical relationships like this use all kinds of removable collars, locks, ropes, or binding devices. She had no need for those things, even though the idea appealed to each of us. The reality was, real control comes from not needing ropes, collars or anything else.

Occasionally, she blindfolded me to heighten the mystery, or the sensation she wanted me to feel, or perhaps to display to others watching the level of control she had over me with the symbol of the rope or handcuffs. In reality, she didn't need them. They were for show, for fun, but not a requirement.

What I wanted and asked for is some type of permanent mark. A cut on my chest or perhaps a brand burnt into my arm. Something that hurt deeply and then healed and can never be removed. I wanted this to remind me of where I was when she found me, in pain, wounded, enraged. She healed me, tamed me, brought the power she was born with to bear against my insanity, and cooled the fires of my self-destructive lashing out against a world that did not understand. To be a sub male is no easy thing, surrounded by women who misunderstand your rage as dominance. It was amazingly frustrating. Athena refused to burn me or mark me, but that didn't lessen the need. She said I didn't need it, she knew she owned me, and that should be enough. Perhaps she was correct, she usually was.

EIGHTEEN
THE HOTEL SUB

Athena traveled a lot. She was a paid information technology consultant for a major corporation, and we left the mountain home about once every six weeks to travel from one place to another. She considered these trips opportunities to take risks and display her dominance of me.

This week, we were traveling to a site in Denver, Colorado where she was overseeing the transition of a help desk. I picked her up from work when the day was over and brought her to the room we were staying in. Later, we went to dinner at one of her favorite restaurants in the area. It was called BJ's, a sports bar with amazing pizza, and they also sell one of our favorite wines; Ravenswood Zinfandel, 2010. It pairs amazingly well with a lot of food and it goes especially well with the different pizzas they serve. We ate there and at a few other nearby restaurants, like Quaker Steak. The food at both places is good but we liked BJ's much more. However, on some days when we got back to the hotel room, she didn't like to go out to eat and ordered room service.

Tonight, she came back from work tired and immediately jumped in the shower. She came out of the bathroom wearing the hotel-provided white terry cloth bathrobe, picking up the hotel's menu for room service and after a few minutes of browsing the menu, she called down and ordered a chicken cordon bleu dish with crab bisque on the side. She asked how long until it would be delivered. The hotel room service said it would be about ten to fifteen minutes. Athena said that will be perfect.

She walked around the room for a moment, drying her hair and checking the programming on the television. Then she went into the bathroom and came out with a medium sized hand towel. She opened the door to the hotel room and rolled up the towel, placing it in front of the open door to prevent it from closing. Athena walked to the couch that was directly in front of the open door. I watched all of these preparations from the only chair in the room. She sat down on the couch and smiled at me.

Spreading her legs and assuming an instantly assertive air she said, "Edge, my little bitch, I'd like you to put on a show for room service. The server will be up here in about ten minutes. I'd like them to arrive with the food while you go down on me. Be a good bitch now, and don't disappoint me."

I rose from the chair and got down on my knees in front of her spread legs. Slowly, I worked my way into her, starting to kiss the insides of her thighs and stroke her soft shin. In a few moments, I was slipping my tongue inside of her, exploring what would give her pleasure today. Sometimes she liked to be gentle and soft, while other times she would grind her pussy against me so violently and for so long, I was afraid I'd pass out from not being able to breathe. In BDSM culture, it is quite common and is considered a form of humiliation. I have to admit as frightening as it is to not be able to breathe, I do enjoy the frantic animalistic thrusting and being deprived of air until she finally comes. She was grinding me hard today and occasionally, I heard people walking past in the hallway outside of our open door. They made comments as she ground on me and cried out. One woman remarked that it was disgusting and a few moments later, a male voice said "Damn, that's fucking hot."

Then I heard a knock, and an unsure voice said, "Excuse me, did you order room service?"

Athena said, "Yes I did, come in please."

Now that she had an audience, she didn't slow down her frantic thrusts and instead, they got faster and more urgent. She asked the person who had brought the food to leave it on the coffee table. I barely heard the cart being pushed into the room and the sound of the plates, glasses, and silverware being laid out. I focused on how much longer until she came and how much longer I could go without air. Finally, she arched her back in an explosive pelvic thrust and a passionate involuntary gasp of air into her lungs. She released me and allowed me to breathe.

I sucked in air as fast as I could and heard a female voice say, "Man, you guys are intense!"

I looked up and saw a Hispanic woman in her late twenties standing next to the food cart. We were her last stop on this run of room service. She smiled at Athena and said, "How do you get him to be so enthusiastic?"

Athena explained my status as her property, and that I serve her. The two women talked for a few moments, ignoring me. My task was complete and they no longer found me interesting. The woman asked about the relationship and appeared interested in the dynamics of Athena's role as owner of me. I listened to them speaking as I went into the bathroom to wash off the cum covering my face. When I returned, Athena and the room service girl were closing the door to the room.

Athena said, "You thought you were done, didn't you?" I stopped mid-stride and she continued. "No bitch, you're not done yet. My friend here wants to spend time with you on your knees in front of her, in exchange for the tip I was going to leave. On your knees bitch, you'll take whatever she gives you while I eat dinner and watch."

I was uncertain what to expect from the woman but she enthusiastically shed her uniform pants and shirt, and sat back in the chair I used earlier. The woman was nearly naked, leaving only her bra on, and she opened her legs to me. She pulled open the lips of her pussy and said to me, "You'll start right here!"

This is surreal to most of you reading this. It is surprising how many people are open to the idea in the real world if you simply open the door and allow it to occur.

She was musky and sweaty as I slipped my tongue inside her. Nowhere near as quiet as Athena, she rode me enthusiastically and directed me. She was much more verbal in her direction and I enjoyed her response to my exploration of her ass and pussy. She came not once, twice, but three times in what felt like a very short period of time. Her need was intoxicating as she crossed back and forth between outbursts of Spanish and English, starting to build up for a fourth orgasm, pumping her hips rapidly as she ground her clit against my pursed lips. One hand held the back of my head while the other hand grabbed her raven black hair and pulled it back as she arched her back. In a final carnal cry of pleasure, she came, her entire body rigid, all her muscles contracted and tense as she used me to exploit and extract every bit of ecstasy she had earned.

As she finally returned mentally back to the room, Athena said to me, "Well done, bitch! That was amazing to watch."

I felt used to a depth and darkness that I had not felt since I had been the fuck toy for Bliss and Athena, passed back and forth between them as property to be used. The depth of this need to be used as property and exploited as a sexual toy is hard to explain, it is however very real, and very hard to find a woman that understands it.

I stood and cleaned up again, feeling amazingly happy, healed and like I had a purpose. As I came back out of the bathroom, the Hispanic woman was nearly dressed. She made no attempt to look at me or acknowledge me but thanked Athena for allowing her to use me. Looking in the mirror, she straightened her hair and uniform, and then pushed the cart to the door.

She turned to Athena and said, "My name is Miranda by the way. If you'd like me to bring you room service again you can request me."

"Thank you Miranda, I'm sure we'll be happy to order room service again the next time we stay here. We're leaving early tomorrow morning but we do come here often."

The women smiled at each other, hugged briefly and Miranda left the room. I settled next to Athena and started to eat my order of food, amazed at how satisfying the food could be after being used by the hotel staff.

Not every trip was like this. On another trip, we went to a bed and breakfast for a change of pace. After we settled in, Athena wanted to get drinks before dinner. The bed and breakfast had a small pub and restaurant so we stopped there before dinner. The bartender doubled as wait staff when the flow of patrons was slow. He came to our table just as Athena removed her jacket, revealing a shear delicate blouse. It barely obscured her dark erect nipples and the full sensuous curves of her breasts. As usual, Athena was confident and self-assured as she asked for a menu, pretending not to notice the bartender's fixation on her breasts. She ordered and stared directly at the bartender as he tried unsuccessfully to keep his eyes on hers.

When he left our table, she said, "So, tell me how it feels to watch him stare at my nipples."

I told her the range of emotions that crossed my mind watching this man barely contain his desire to fuck her right there on the table in front of me. He frequently visited our table and repeatedly tried to strike up a conversation with her. I wasn't even on his radar as he complimented her on the blouse. She smiled and said thank you, her eyes staring directly at him, daring him to continue the conversation as she pulled her shoulders slightly back, making her already turgid nipples strike out even more under the sheer fabric. The man was beside himself with lust. I was a mere observer in this flirtatious web she wove with the now obviously aroused bartender.

He suggested we take dinner in the bar and that he would be happy to bring us our meals from the kitchen. Athena thanked him while absent-mindedly stroking her right nipple with a flick of her crossed left hand. The way she played the man was masterful and really quite arousing to watch as her property. I was unsure how far she would take this and I suppose that was the point. She not only sexually controlled the randy bartender, but she controlled me as well. Never knowing how far she would go reasserting her ownership of me, the tension was incredibly addictive. I never knew who would end up in the room on these trips. It was unnerving how well she understood this dark unspoken and twisted need to be owned.

We returned to the room, which was on the first floor of the bed and breakfast directly across from the pub. After getting ready for bed, I fell asleep quickly and seemingly only a few moments later, Athena opening the door to our room woke me up. She was completely nude and stood in the doorway, staring across the courtyard at the soon to be closed pub. It was now 1:00 a.m. and the bed and breakfast was quiet. She stood in the door until finally, the bartender looked up from his closing duties and saw her.

She said to me, "Edge, are you awake?"

I replied, "I am."

"Let's give the bartender a show. Turn on the lights to our room while I prop the door open."

Our bed was directly in front of the now propped open door. Athena guided me to the bed, directing me much like a conductor directs a symphony, expertly managing me and telling what she wanted the bartender to watch me do to her.

She said a few moments later, "We definitely have an audience, bitch. Make me proud of you!"

I did my best and hoped she was satisfied. Finally, she got up, turned off the light, closed and locked the door. Coming back to bed, she was laughing.

I giggled and asked, "Why are you laughing?"

"You should have seen the look on his face when he realized the show was over, and that was all he'd ever get from us. He looked devastated."

I laughed too, having seen the look on many men when Athena was finished with them. I was glad I was not one of them and I admit a little bit frightened that someday I might be.

NINETEEN
THE GREEN TURTLE

Occasionally, we both traveled to the east coast for various commit-ments. This particular trip, we were both away from home but in different locations. I was at Aberdeen Proving grounds in Maryland. Athe-na was at Fort Benning, Georgia for training. We communicated by text message and phone calls daily. Eventually, she arranged to meet me in at the Baltimore Airport. Her flight arrived late in the day.

Night fell as I arrived at the parking lot and headed to the terminal, waiting for her to come through security. It rains a lot more in Maryland than Colorado, and the change was nice. It was just starting to rain when I got out of the car and entered the airport. Escalators took me from the top floor of the parking lot to the main floor of the terminal. I watched people meeting family members and grabbing luggage as I rode the escala-tor downward. When I arrived at the main floor, I went to the stairway she would be coming down and waited, wondering apprehensively what she had planned for me, how she would reassert her dominance of me when she arrived.

Scenarios flipped through my head as I waited, wondering what she would wear, if she'd changed her hair. Would she even want me to serve her anymore? Perhaps she had found another more capable servant. I tried not to think about that. The fear of being lost again without her was a constant nagging sore I tried not to pick at. When we had been separated as long as we had on this trip, the feelings were near panic.

Athena texted me that she had just landed as I sat in a Starbucks coffee shop, watching people walking past. She said that she had to change her clothes in the restroom and then she would be right out. I smiled, my heart pounding because I knew it was about to begin. Finally, to feel safe again. To feel her ownership. It may be hard to understand the peace that this brought me. It took me forever to understand it myself. No matter what relationship I was in, I could never find peace until I was finally taken, dominated and owned by this woman. I was lost in my thoughts and suddenly, there she was standing in front of me.

With a knowing, strangely powerful smile, she said, "Hi bitch, did you miss me?"

Immediately, I felt the strength of her presence. "Bitch" to anyone else would be an insult. For us, it was an affirmation of our continued commitment. I was now and always will be her bitch, she has told me that and much more with the statement. I grinned broadly and bowed my head, embarrassed at how deeply I needed her and how incredibly happy I was to see her again.

Her change of clothing was not lost on me, as I saw why she could not wear the sheer black dress on the plane. She was clearly naked under the dress. A guy walking past us collided with another man as he turned to stare at her. We laughed and she sat down next to me.

She said, "I'd like a drink as well, bitch. Get me one while I sit here."

I ordered her favorite Starbucks drink, a Green Tea Latte, and returned. She stared unapologetically at me and said nothing. Wave upon wave of dominance and sexuality rolled from her, reminding me of the control she had over me almost immediately so many years ago. I waited until she was ready to go and then carried her bags as she walked ahead of me to the escalator. She stood one step above me on the escalator, looking ahead and then behind us as we started to ascend the stairway.

She said, "I think you'd have already been licking my ass by now, bitch. What's taking so long?"

I looked behind us and unbelievably, no one was there. The airport was barely occupied due to the hour so nobody was watching.

My face was pressed up against her ass moments later, my tongue getting reacquainted with her scent and flavor. How we pulled this off without getting arrested, I don't know but we did. Once we were on the second floor and heading to the parking lot, she stepped onto the moving walkway. There were three women in front of us, all standing in one spot, choosing to let the walkway transport them along.

Athena said to me, just loud enough for them to hear, "On your knees and eat me right now."

There was no hesitation. I dropped and slipped my tongue inside her, pressing hard against her, pulling her to me, both hands firmly holding her naked ass as I ground my face against her. I heard the women commenting.

One said, "That's disgusting!"

One of the others said, "I wish my husband were that disgusting."

Then another commented, "Jesus, what I would not give for my boyfriend to want me like that."

Athena laughed at their comments. Finally, she said, "You can get up now. We're nearing the end of the walkway."

I got up with the three strangers looking at me. Athena took my hand and said, "Come with me," quietly leaving no doubt to anyone watching us who was in control.

We walked to the rental car and I opened her door, closing it after she slipped in the front seat. I put her luggage into the trunk. The drive back to the Aberdeen area took us past a tollbooth. About a half-mile from the booth, she stripped off her dress, leaned over, unzipped my pants and said, "Try to pretend like nothing unusual is going on."

I was in her mouth and nearly lost control of the vehicle before I regained my vision. The intensity of her technique was unbelievable. As I approached the booth, there were only two lanes open. I picked the one on the right and pulled up. As I slowed down, she started moaning loudly and raised her ass up.

She said, "I want to feel your fingers in me while you pay the toll."

I slipped two of my fingers inside her ass and she cried out. Then feverishly, she was back on my cock, sliding her hand up and down the wet shaft, looking up at me as she licked the tip. The toll was manned by a middle aged woman who was instantly disgusted at the sexual display.

I paid her and gave thanks as Athena said loud enough for the woman to hear, "God, I want to taste your cum."

The woman cringed as we drove away. Moments later, Athena stopped tormenting me and said, "That was fun. What was her reaction?"

I explained, "She was less than pleased."

We both laughed. Athena put the sheer dress back on, saying she was hungry.

She said, "Sucking cock always makes me ravenous. Where can we go eat?"

I remembered some of the people I was here with had been going to a sports bar called the Green Turtle and I suggested it. I had been there twice. They have decent seafood and since it was the weekend, there would be a band. Usually the band was really good. Athena liked the idea.

We arrived about an hour later. Athena was in her element; the Turtle was full of men and women who were instantly drawn to her. We took a seat and in five minutes, a woman came over and asked if she knew Athena from somewhere. She was clearly hitting on her, attracted to the blatant display of dominance and sexuality Athena made entering the restaurant in the sheer black dress. The two women talked like they were old friends and the stranger left Athena a business card with her name and personal cell phone number written on the back. We smiled and laughed to each other about the conversation she had with the woman.

It was a verbal dry humping right there in the booth we sat in. Busboys came by our table often and our beverage glasses never reached half empty. Amazing how the service improved when Athena was present. She flirted with several of the wait staff and a woman across the restaurant from us. The woman stared at her, unblinking and unashamed. They gazed at each other for some time, making "I wanna fuck you" eyes at each other. Athena went to the rest room just before we left and the woman followed her in. Ten minutes later, they emerged arm in arm, laughing and talking like they had known each other for years. I don't know what happened in the restroom. I never asked.

We were getting ready to leave the restaurant and Athena said, "I have something I'd like you to wear."

She reached in her purse and pulled out a leather collar. It was about two inches wide, made of black leather and had rings placed about every two inches apart.

She said, "Put it on now."

I did so and instantly people were looking at us. She got up calmly, pulled out a very noticeable dog leash and attached it to the collar.

"That will do nicely, bitch. Come with me."

People pointed and others raised their cell phones up to take a picture. This wasn't something you saw every day I guess. Athena led me to the front desk and paid for the meal. She then walked me out of the restaurant and to the car. I'd parked under a light in the parking lot. Old habits die hard I guess, trying to maximize every advantage should things go to shit. She led me to the car and as we walked, I noticed a hotel that shared the parking lot with the Turtle. A busload of people just pulled up to the hotel and they were getting off the bus as we came to our car.

Athena stopped and said, "What timing!"

She hopped up on the trunk of the White Chevy Monte Carlo we had rented and spread her legs.

"Time for dessert, bitch."

She reeled me in like a fish with the leash. One of the people behind us from the bus commented. It sounded like a man speaking and he said, "There's something that you don't see every day!"

Athena said, "You have an audience now, bitch."

The people from the restaurant and the bus were all watching. The idea was incredibly intense and I like that she made me perform in front of others. I stayed focused on giving her whatever she needed while she entertained the spectators with her control of me. She did her best to show her dominance and ended it with a fistful of my hair in her hand while she ground my face on her. She loudly repeated "This is what you need isn't it, bitch?" over and over.

Finally, she finished and allowed me to get up and open the car door for her. I got in as well and we headed to our room. It was late and I thought the night was done, well at least I thought she was finished with her display of me. I was wrong.

TWENTY
BOSTON

We were in Boston for an academic conference that Athena had submitted two papers to, both were accepted, and she was presenting them to the entire conference. I accompanied her as usual. We stayed in a five star hotel about a half an hour from the conference. Athena always liked to stay at a hotel with a well equipped gym. She did this for several reasons. First, she liked me to work out constantly, demanded it actually. I had to work out as hard as possible to maintain the type of physique she demanded. It wasn't something I minded at all, since I have always liked to work out, but now the reason was different. I used to work out for the sheer enjoyment of it. Now I worked out to maintain a certain level of physicality, fitness, and look she admired. I had to watch what I ate carefully and balance cardio with weights to achieve what she desired. Second, Athena had chosen this hotel for its attractive lounge and lobby.

When we arrived, she immediately prepared for the next day. She had one last dry run to do on the presentation slides and her talk. While she prepared, I unpacked all her clothing, put her shoes in the closet, hung her clothing up, and laid out her toiletries for the morning. There was a specific order to which she wanted me to adhere. I placed her clothing and bathroom items so that no matter what hotel we were in, she felt familiarity in the room. It was a routine she had trained me well to perform every trip I accompanied her.

As I unpacked her clothing, I noticed some very short boy shorts she had brought to work out in. Athena would be showing off the entire time we worked out in the morning. The shorts barely covered her ass and after a few minutes on any exercise machine, they had crept up just the way she preferred, to show off her body. She let the shorts ride up as much as possible at the back and the front, as she bent over in front of whatever male or female happened to be in the gym. Athena loved making a point out of being as sexual and seductive as possible in the hotels we stayed at, especially in the gym. Morning workouts could be quite interesting for the onlookers.

After the workout, we left the gym. Hungry eyes followed us out of the door and down the hallway. Athena didn't pretend she didn't notice, she was well aware of the tension in the room. We walked to the elevator and she pushed the button, calling it to our floor. She grinned at me, wiped the sweat that had beaded on her forehead with a towel and pulled me to her as the deep bumping noise that sounded from the elevator shaft announced the arrival of the car.

"I believe we have an audience, my willing bitch. When we get in the elevator, I want you to be on your knees."

We both looked back at the gym and there were several people still watching the ongoing show she had been providing. The elevator door opened and several people exited to go to the gym. Athena held the door open and stopped it from closing or going back up to another floor. I entered the elevator and dropped to my knees; a position I admit I preferred. It means I would be used in some way…whatever way she desired.

Athena had me face sideways in the elevator so that onlookers had a clear view. Before she stepped into the elevator, she faced away from the gym and bending over, she stripped off the very short boy shorts she had been barely wearing. I imagined the view of her perfect ass and swollen pussy that the onlookers from the gym had.

My eyes were suddenly very heavy. Submission to her was a drug to which I was addicted, and these public displays were submission on steroids. I really craved the way this felt to have her display how I serve her at her choosing. She stepped into the elevator, still holding the door and faced away from me. With her left hand, she pulled me into her and started to grind her ass against my eager face. My tongue danced across her ass and pussy, and she started to grind harder and faster. Her right hand held the door, while her left hand pressed harder and harder against the back of my head. I couldn't see anything so she told me what she saw.

"We have an audience. The entire gym is watching me grind my ass in your face. Stay on your knees until I'm finished."

She finally allowed the door to close and said, "You'll remain there until I tell you to get up."

Athena pushed each of the buttons on the elevator's control panel, ensuring that the door would open at least eight times before we reached the floor our room was on. On the first floor, the door opened and I heard the voices of a male and a female, and then silence as they watched her grinding her ass against me. I had craved this feeling for days. I couldn't get enough of her ownership.

She described what they looked like and the surprise on their faces.

"When the door opens next, if someone is there, I want you to use your hands and spread my ass wide. Let them see you lick my ass."

The door opened and I heard many male voices. Instead of them staying outside the elevator, they got on. Athena stepped to the nearest wall of the elevator and put one leg up on the rail. She pulled my head in between her legs and shoved her pussy against me, slowly at first and then faster and faster, grinding and rotating her hips. They watched my every move as they rode the elevator to the next floor, laughing at the expression on my face as I slipped my tongue deep into her pussy while she came in a final long intense shudder. She encouraged me to go deeper and I forced my tongue as far into her as I could. The door opened and they all got off, laughing and making comments about how that was something you don't see every day. Several of them took pictures of us with their cell phones and promised they would post them on the web. Moments later, the door closed again.

"How did that make you feel, to have all those men watching you lick my pussy like a dog in heat, my hungry little bitch?"

I admitted it felt really good to be owned this way. A woman stood outside the elevator on the next floor and she was alarmed at first but then intrigued. She asked if she could get on the elevator with us.

Athena replied as she breathed heavily, "Please do."

The woman remained quiet at first and just watched as Athena ground against me, maneuvering me and making me lick her exactly how and where she wanted.

Athena pulled my head from her and said to me, "Tell our guest who owns you."

I told her, "Every day, I serve Athena in whatever way she wishes."

The woman replied, "I want a man to serve me like this."

Athena said, "He's very lucky he finally realized he was born for this. It took some work to get him here, but now he submits as he should." Athena asked me, "Do you want to continue licking my pussy?"

"Yes please."

The woman handed Athena a business card. "I'll be in the hotel for a couple of days. Let's get together and have a drink."

The doors opened and she exited the elevator. Finally, we arrived at our floor and I got up off the floor. My face was covered in her musky sweat and cum. I smelled like her ass and it was intoxicating.

Athena pulled on her boy shorts and said, "Shall we?"

I walked off the elevator and down the hallway to our room. My mind spun from the rush of being dominated in such a public manner. It was a drug for me and I was an addict.

The next day, the conference began at 9:00 a.m. It was held at Boston College in the Corcoran Commons building. We walked upstairs to the Heights room and checked in. There was an hour at the beginning to allow everyone to check in and get settled. It was a "techie conference," with experts from all over the world presenting papers on various subjects. I carried all of her stuff to the conference and we got settled in for a long day of academics pontificating on how amazing they are in their particular field. I listened and occasionally, there was an interesting subject or talk.

The day passed quickly and lunch arrived. The college provided sandwiches made in the cafeteria downstairs and they were surprisingly good. All during the first day, Athena watched the other people at the conference and made mental notes. She was deciding which people she would like to collaborate with on future projects, and which people to avoid. Occasionally, I saw her check her watch or cellular phone, noting the time. At first, I didn't notice the pattern to this and then I saw she was checking to see when other women left to use the restroom. It puzzled me but I knew from experience everything she did had a purpose. I'd find out later what that purpose was, if she wanted me to know.

Athena saw that I noticed her behavior and she gave me a knowing smile. She was pleased, I suppose, at my continued situational awareness. I had already checked everyone in the room visually for weapons, and assessed if anything went wrong, if one of the eggheads was not what or who they appeared to be, where we would exit. No one here was a threat to anyone, except maybe a devoted Republican. God help a conservative who entered this room! Regardless, this was my area of awareness and it was safe for her to be here.

Her awareness of the time and the people coming and going from the conference continued to puzzle me. It occupied my mind during a rather boring presentation on the digital identification we have all left on the web...*yawn*!

The day passed and the conference was over. We returned to our hotel and later ate dinner at a very good Japanese restaurant called The Yamato. They have excellent sushi and the service was great. The next day, the conference restarted and at break, we went for a tour of the college. If you have never been to Boston College and get the chance to go there, I recommend it. The grounds are immaculate and the structures and buildings are amazing.

We toured the grounds and ended up in an old library that our guide told us gets a lot more use since the Harry Potter movies because of its similarity to Hogwarts. We all laughed at this as we entered the library. The building was unbelievable. Nothing at Harvard compared to Boston College as far as the grounds and how well kept and beautiful it all was. As we toured the building, Athena took my hand and guided me skillfully to the back of the pack of academics. I saw the look in her eyes and knew she had something planned, which would be risky and amazing. My heart pounded and the heaviness started to build in my eyes. I tried to act interested in the tour but something much more interesting was coming.

As soon as our guide reached the far end of the stained glass windows, she was babbling on aimlessly. Apparently, each window represented a discipline the Jesuit priest felt needed to be represented. She headed back up towards an older part of the library that housed volumes of manuscripts written by Jesuit priests in the past. Athena pushed me into a small nook just a few feet from the group. The group was so close I could hear the heavy breathing of a few of the more out of shape members.

Athena held her finger up to her lips and made a "shhh" sound. She pulled out a chair and sat facing the open area where the students would normally sit to study. As she removed the black thong she wore under her grey skirt, I smiled and automatically dropped to my knees. The sensations were incredible. The risk was high for us. If caught, we'd be on the evening news. (We have only been caught once, in a dark theater many years ago…it was worth it!)

She was wet from anticipation and ferociously ground against me, gasping quietly as she reached a very intense and enthusiastic climax a mere arm's length from the unaware academics. I got up and kept her underwear in my pocket, playfully refusing to return them to her.

We rejoined the group and they were none the wiser one of them just experienced a very intense oral sex session provided by her more than willing servant. After exiting the rear of the building, we pretended to be interested in the concrete labyrinth in the courtyard outside our guide showed to us. She then took us back to the conference room. We smiled and laughed as we walked back to the Heights room. The secret we shared and the risk we had taken made the day seem brighter for both of us. My eyes were heavy from the endorphins and my muscles trembled from the adrenaline surging through my veins.

Athena squeezed my hand and whispered to me, "You're an amazing pool boy!"

The reality was just the opposite. I served an exceptional woman.

On the fourth day, the conference began just like all the rest. Athena presented her papers and seemed a little nervous. I had her laptop and electronics in a backpack.

An hour or so before the time she was scheduled to present, she got up and said to me, "I'll be right back." She said this loud enough for everyone at the table to hear.

Athena walked off casually and a few moments later, she sent me a text. She wanted me to meet her in the women's bathroom. I entered the bathroom quietly and she was waiting for me naked, sitting on the counter, legs spread.

She looked at me with her eyes on fire and said, "I really need to be fucked hard, right here right now. I've been keeping track and every woman in the conference has been to the restroom this hour, so we have about thirty minutes. Make it memorable pool boy, pound me."

I did what my mistress commanded, losing the backpack and hoping she was right about the time frame. She pulled off my shirt and I dropped my pants. I couldn't help but gasp as I slid easily into her. She was so wet and eager. Normally, she'd be careful and quiet, but not this time. Athena was loud and vulgar, and dug her nails into me over and over as she cried out, "Fuck me as hard as you can! Yes! Yes!"

I was sure we'd be caught but rational thought left the building when I found her naked and clearly anxious to be fucked. Somehow, someway, she was right again and we finished much later. She forced me to clean up after, quickly and without protest, stroking my head and complimenting me. Athena was very proud of me as I looked up from between her cleaned pussy.

She returned a few moments later to the conference where I was already seated, carrying two Diet Cokes, one for each of us.

She said, "You look thirsty!"

During her presentation a few minutes later, she gave me a knowing smile as I listened. Again, no one here knew what we had been doing right under their noses. Juvenile? Yes, most definitely and a rush as well. I was one happy pool boy.

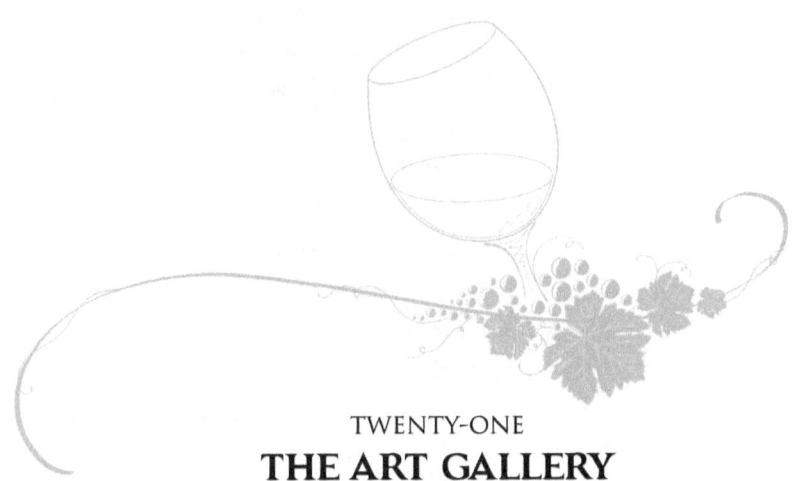

TWENTY-ONE

THE ART GALLERY

Almost always when we traveled to a new place, Athena had me look in the area for an art gallery. She was a rabid fan of Rodin. We were traveling back to Maryland and I mentioned we had time to visit the Baltimore Museum of Art. She was very excited about being able to see another of his works, as the museum had one of the original copies made by Rodin himself in the early 1900s. She had told me in the past how each sculpture was similar but unique in its own way, and to make sure that seeing the sculpture became the focus of my efforts while we were in Baltimore. Athena had business to attend to and this would be my job, making sure that we saw this copy of *The Thinker*.

During the flight there, she recalled the history of the sculpture. The details she retained were incredible. She knew exactly how many copies Rodin personally supervised the production of, and where each of the twenty-eight copies were currently housed. I was a bit overwhelmed by the amount of information she had in her memory about any given subject. There was a reason she was so entrancing to everyone she met, not only was she physically beautiful, but the mind and intellect she possessed was equally remarkable.

When we arrived in Baltimore, I called the museum and verified they would be open. I was alarmed to learn they'd be closed on Monday and

Tuesday, leaving only Wednesday to see the sculpture. We would leave Thursday. This was a very serious error on my part. I hadn't checked the museum's hours before we left, assuming they'd be open.

I took a deep breath, relieved I wouldn't have to explain to Athena I had made a huge mistake not looking into the museum's hours beforehand. Disappointing her wasn't something I took lightly. It was my place to serve her and provide her with the most enjoyable experience I could. To make such a mistake, as this would be very disappointing to her, I would pay dearly. Fortunately, we were able to attend the museum without any additional embarrassing failures on my part.

We parked a distance away and walked up to the museum. As we approached the building, Athena commented on the Roman temple style architecture. She told me casually, as if it were common knowledge, that the style of architecture emphasized the front of the building with a *portico*, or porch as it translated into English. She said that the portico was the entrance to the building, with the roof supported by several columns.

My head swam. Honestly, this kind of constant display of how incredible she was and how she thought made me want to drop to my knees right there on the portico, begging her to grind her pussy in my face. I tried not to make a fool out of myself but the mental image of doing just that took its toll. She saw the distant glassy look in my eyes and instantly knew I was in fantasyland. It happened all the time.

She said, "Let me guess…where you are?"

I smiled weakly. She grabbed my hand, firmly saying, "Come with me. It's time to see your first Rodin."

She was very excited and I shook off my submissive needs, reminding myself how important this was to her.

The statue was incredible, truly incredible. We walked the halls of the museum and looked at the paintings of Henri Matisse, Picasso, Van Gogh, and Renoir. At each painting, we stopped and she described the history of the painter, and some of the pieces themselves. Surprisingly, she didn't know the history of each and was happy to learn more about them. She told me the reason this museum was so remarkably rich in its artworks was largely due to the donations of two sisters, Claribel and Etta Cone.

I sighed and smiled, as all I could think about was how lucky I was to be her property. Of all the women in this world I have met in the course of my life, none matched her ability to make me want, no, desperately need to serve. She was remarkable, and I was fortunate to be able to be her property.

We left Maryland the next morning and traveled all day to return to our mountain home. In the airport before we left, she was on her cell phone to a friend who was an art teacher at a nearby university. They were talking about the paintings and the sculpture. I was listening and suddenly Athena smiled at me.

She said she had an idea and whispered, "I'll be right back."

I sat and watched as she walked out of earshot and excitedly talked to her friend. I didn't know what they are talking about but the animated way she was talking and gesturing with her arms told me that she was very enthusiastic about the idea. She started to walk back to me and I heard her say, "Let's plan on it. Saturday? Great! See you then!"

Athena said, "I have a surprise for you!"

I couldn't wait. Her surprises were always something she instinctively knew I'd enjoy and need. The anticipation built as I counted down the days until Saturday.

Saturday arrived and we got up early to work out. Athena packed a bag for us to take on the mystery trip she had planned. I made breakfast as usual while she typed an address into the GPS app on her smart phone. A few minutes later, we were on our way.

She said to me, "Follow the directions, Edge."

A couple of hours later, we arrived at our destination: The Art Institute of Colorado in Denver. We parked the car in a parking lot and walked to the building her friend had asked to meet us in. Athena was giddy and laughing like a little girl, telling me that she knew I was going to love the surprise she had in store for me. I have to admit, I was a little mystified. We had attended art galleries all over the nation but I had never seen her this excited.

We met her friend and they exchanged hugs. Athena whispered in the woman's ear briefly and I realized they were co-conspirators in this "surprise." Her friend took us to a room and then left.

Giving me a playful smile she said, "We'll see you two in a few minutes."

Then she disappeared. Athena told me to disrobe and put all of my clothes in a bag she had brought. She undressed as well and handed me a robe to wear, then she put one on herself.

"Come with me now."

We walked down a short hallway and into a large auditorium filled with students...art students. The instructor was addressing the class and told them today, they were to capture the bond exhibited by these two models. She explained to the class that we were friends of hers and that we would be modeling a Dominate female and her worshipping submissive male. My head swam. I looked at Athena and she smiled at me.

"I remembered the look in your eyes at the art gallery in Maryland, and I wanted to give you this gift. Today, we'll be live models for my friend's art class. Now remove your robe and serve me."

I removed my robe as she removed hers. I got on my knees in front of her and she stood over me. Looking down into my eyes, she placed a leg over my shoulder and pulled me into her. I did what she directed me to do for the rest of the day. Occasionally, we changed positions, or took a break for a drink or whatever we needed, but we returned quickly to the class and assumed another position, displaying her dominance and my willing submission.

I looked at the class occasionally to see their reaction as I continually caressed, fondled, and licked her, stroking her thighs during momentary breaks in the oral servitude. She was too sensitive to be orally stimulated for the whole day. The entire day was a display of her ownership of me. Finally, she finished the class sitting in a chair, legs spread wide, two hands on my head as she ground against me desperately. She finally came and lay back in the chair, breathing heavily, as I continued at a gentler pace.

The class ended as the teacher thanked us for our time. We put the robes back on and returned to the dressing room. I was amazed at the way this felt, the way she understood my needs at such an instinctive and visceral level. Only she could understand what a gift this really was to me.

Later we were home, sitting on the front porch, drinking a bottle of Geneseo Cabernet Sauvignon, listening to Joan Sutherland ("The Flower Duet" is my favorite piece). She told me to explain every thought and emotion I felt during the day. I had to relive the whole experience for her and tried to explain as best as I could that only in moments like today, where she put me on display undeniably as her property did I feel truly complete. I had finally found what I was looking for and she continued to show me how deeply this went into my soul. There was no denying who we both were.

Several months later, Athena told me it was our turn to host the Wine Club. Each member took their turn at providing a wine to focus on and share with the group. Athena decided to host a trip to a local art gallery. There was a young female artist from Colorado who had been discovered by a wealthy admirer. The sponsor had rented a gallery to display the artist and her works. Athena had decided the club was going to the gallery first and then to our home to share the wine she had chosen.

We all arrived and I discovered she had contacted the wealthy sponsor and explained our club would be attending. The sponsor had politely closed the exhibit to everyone but us for two hours. As we entered, Athena turned to me and smiled. There was a playful hint in her smile that told me there was more to this viewing of art than I had been told. I thought she had plans for me in some closet, or hidden nook of the gallery.

We browsed the works of art, paintings, and sketches. Some I liked and some I didn't. Athena commented on certain techniques the artist used and explained the differences to me. Then she led me to a room that housed several pieces. The room was separate from the rest of the artwork and had an informative handout explaining the pieces. The theme of the room was "A Promise Fulfilled." As I entered, I was speechless. It was us, Athena and I, from the day at the Art Institute modeling for the class. The artist had captured Athena beautifully in all her power and dominance. I was mesmerized by the power and intensity of the drawings. Additionally, she'd captured my need and willingness to serve Athena in such a way that I felt proud and yet ashamed. Proud I belonged to her, ashamed I wasn't worthy of her. Only a submissive can understand the duality of emotions you feel when you are truly owned.

We sat back and watched as the Wine Club members took turns entering the room and looking at the sketches. Some were intrigued, others disgusted. One or two viewed the sketches and then glanced at us, saying nothing but noticing the resemblance. Athena's eyes were on fire as she watched our Wine Club members smiling, asking for each member's thoughts of the drawings. Later, we shared our latest wine find with the club and discussed the drawings. She flashed a secret co-conspirator's smile to me across the room as we talked in small groups in the house. Again, she had given me another gift: showing the world her pride in owning me, her property.

Later that night, as we lay in bed, I thought back to the first time I was at her apartment so many years ago.

"Do you remember that day? The day you first made me tuna steaks?"

Athena turned off the computer she was working on and said, "Yes, I do."

I continued, "I remember you made me tell you how I felt, what I was thinking. It was hard to do but it felt good to finally admit it." She smiled. I said, "What I am curious about is, what were you thinking? You never said much except to tell me what I was, and I would be doing. May I ask what you were thinking?"

She stared at me again like she did that day. "I was sizing you up, testing you. I've never met a male who so desperately needed to serve a woman, and so stubbornly fought it. With every breath you were in conflict, every emotion was painful to you. All I could see was pain and you had no idea how to be what you were born to be. I saw raw potential in you. I had to be sure of what I was seeing. Then I realized you were already mine. You had no choice. I owned you and all I had to do was make it clear to you."

We looked at each other for a long time, quietly taking in the changes that had occurred in each of us. I was very lucky to be the property of such an amazing woman.

TWENTY-TWO
GRADUATION

S everal years of work and effort were about to come to an end. Athena
was going to graduate soon from a local university with her doctorate.
She had worked hard and long to achieve this goal and I had done what
I could to support her since we met years ago. Some things had changed,
some hadn't. We were more comfortable with each other and our roles in
this relationship. More honest, more real. I guess all relationships evolve
and ours had as well. She told me she had a task for me to complete at
graduation and that I needed to be well groomed and immaculately clean
before the ceremonies. This puzzled me but as usual, I did as I was told,
curious what she had planned for me. This day was her day, her celebra-
tion. I was there to take pictures of the ceremony. I had no degree and
honestly, had no desire to get one. I knew my place and what I was.

Anyway, we arrived at the enormous convention center that would
house the graduation. The Belco Theater in the Colorado Convention
Center was where the graduation would be held in downtown Denver. It
was an enormous building and there were thousands of graduates in the
building several hours before the actual ceremony would begin. I dropped
Athena off at the door and it took several minutes to locate parking near
the convention center. The graduation was much larger than I realized.
The school she had attended the past three years had students in atten-

dance worldwide taking virtual classes. Some had been able to maintain attendance through civil wars in their countries; the Arab Spring as it was called had been unable to deter them in obtaining degrees. It was quite amazing to realize how important education was to their future.

I entered the building and texted Athena. Trying to locate her in this enormous building without texting or calling would take hours. She told me she was near the theater and gave me directions how to meet her. When I was nearly there, several minutes had passed, the building was that big! Athena texted me and said that she had to attend a rehearsal. She instructed me to wait for her at a small café inside the convention center. I waited for about a half an hour, drinking a Diet Pepsi and watching the crowds of people walk past, getting ready to watch the graduation.

Finally, she contacted me about thirty-five minutes later. She told me to meet her near the theater and I returned to the front entrance. She walked up to me giddy and smiling. Finally, this day had come for her and she was excited. I got a brief insight into the little girl she must have been thirty or more years ago. She hugged me and thanked me for being there. I was glad to be here I told her and I meant it.

She said, "Now I need you to follow me without questions."

I nodded and did as she asked. She made small talk as we walked down one long hallway after another. I was disorientated in the building and didn't know where we were anymore. Athena, on the other hand, knew exactly where we were. She stopped me in a deserted hallway, turned me to face her and smiled confidently.

"Edge, I need to you to do what you were born to do. Can you do that for me?"

"Yes," I replied.

Athena removed a blindfold from her purse and placed it across my eyes, tightening it. She said as she tightened the clasps, "I've been emailing other female graduates in the doctoral program to explain that I'm offering them a gift from me to them for graduation. Several women responded that they would much appreciate 'the gift' and we have been coordinating where to get together."

She checked to make sure that I saw nothing at all through the blindfold and said, "You are to be my gift, Edge. You will do as each of them asks."

I instantly became nervous.

"Don't be afraid. I'll be right here, but you will do as they ask, is that clear?"

I paused and finally replied, "Yes, it's clear."

Athena took my hand and walked me to a nearby room. I heard the voices of several different women talking quietly and laughing nervously as I entered the room, directed by my owner. She told me to kneel and guided me to the floor. I was on my knees on some kind of cushion, hands at my sides.

She said in a commanding yet playful tone, "This is my gift to all of you. You are all exceptional women and he is my property. He will serve you as you wish, now, who will be first?"

I heard chatter in several different languages, and wondered how many women were in this room. On one hand, I was filled with anticipation at what I hoped would happen. I was afraid as well, there were a lot of voices and different languages. It was intimidating. There was a pause then I suddenly became aware the space in front of me had changed, someone was there. One hand guided my head down between two legs. A woman sat in a chair in front of me, legs spread, and she slowly ground against my mouth, increasing the pressure and speed of each gyration of her hips as her breathing quickened. She muttered something in a language I didn't recognize as the pace quickened and her inhibitions fell away. Finally, she came and I tasted the change in her as cum filled my mouth. She finished with me and I felt Athena there at my side.

She said quietly, "I'm going to wash you off after each of them is finished with you."

A warm soapy cloth wiped the sticky cum and sweat off my face. Another hand was there and I was once again buried in another complete stranger's wet pussy. She ground harder, much harder, and furiously, hips driving with piston-like thrusting. This was a brutal face fucking like I had never had before and in spite of the ferocity, I admit I was disappointed when it finally ended. Over and over, Athena cleaned me up and it started again.

Maybe on the fifth or sixth woman, it all came to a stop. I sensed a woman standing in front of me and the room fell silent. I heard what Athena later told me was a woman who she described as a more "traditional Domme," which to me meant hardcore. Later Athena told me the woman approached me and glared at me as I knelt on the floor in front of her.

Athena spoke to her in English and the woman returned the conversation in German. Athena spoke German as well as several other languages and so they began to discuss me. Apparently, the German woman felt I wasn't a legitimate submissive, since Athena was not a hardcore Domme.

The two women sparred verbally for a few minutes in German and then Athena said, "Edge, I'd like you to demonstrate to this woman your complete submission to me. Know that I'll be right here, but I want you to keep your hands at your side and do as she demands, is that clear?"

I had been tested this way before, it wasn't always pleasant, and the only real reward was the look in Athena's eyes when it was over, a look of exceptional pride.

I breathed deeply and said, "I am ready."

Athena spoke to the woman and then I felt a hard slap across the face, nearly knocking me to the floor. My face stung and I saw stars. The remaining women in the room began to whisper as I heard a thick German accent directly in front of me.

"You will remember this day, little sub bitch boy."

Wham! She slapped me again on the other side of my face. Someone gasped far back in the room. Still, I stayed on my knees, hands unrestrained at my side. The woman pulled me gruffly into her very bushy cunt and began to grind against me viciously, calling me names and thrusting hard against my already swollen lips and now very sore face. Athena said nothing, but I knew she was there watching, waiting to step in if things got out of hand. Over and over, the German Domme rode me and then slapped my face.

Finally, after several minutes had passed, she reached a ferocious climax and held my head painfully locked between her thighs. I couldn't breathe, I couldn't see, but I knew I couldn't fail Athena by panicking. I waited, focusing on anything but the need to breathe and finally it occurred to me to play this game, I must continue to serve. I started to lick her deeply and almost immediately, her legs opened and she became receptive to me. I could breathe again and took this opportunity to prove myself. I attacked the bushy German cunt with new enthusiasm and soon she came again, this time without striking me.

She got up when she had finished with me and I heard her pulling on her pants. She said something to Athena in German and she disappeared. Later, I asked Athena what she'd said.

"She told me you are a rare find and that I had better keep a tight grip on you, because finding another sub this devoted and skilled would not be easy."

She was very proud of me and it showed in her approving gaze.

I lost count at how many women were there that day. I just did my best to make Athena happy.

Finally Athena said to me, "This one will be the last, Edge."

Familiar legs wrapped around my head and firm strong hands guided me skillfully as I went down on her. She pulled me back, rolled over, and pulled my face into her ass as she rode me, hips rising and falling as she guided me, directed me, and encouraged me to perform. Finally, she came violently and then I heard laughter as she pulled off my blindfold. Athena smiled at me as I looked up at her, still needing more.

"You are such an amazing sub, I am very proud of you today, Edge. Time to graduate!"

I got up and we left the room. An hour later, I sat in the theater and wondered which of the women walking across the stage were in the room. The announcer called Athena's name and she walked confidently across the stage. After receiving her degree and academic hood, she turned to leave the stage. Almost as an afterthought, she held up her degree as she looked directly at me, smiling proudly. It was a very big day for both of us.

Later, outside the auditorium, she introduced me to several people and most of them were women. I looked for a sign that they were smiling, smirking, or hiding something. Not one of them gave anything away. I had no idea if any of them were in the room and I dared not ask Athena. I was her gift; none of this was for me in spite of how much I enjoyed it.

On the way home, Athena got a call on her cell phone. She answered and started a lively conversation with someone on the other end. From what I could gather, catching only her side of the discussion, someone was coming to Colorado next week and asked to see us.

Athena said, "Of course, and please consider staying with us while you are here."

She hung up and turned to me. "Do you remember the woman who gave me her card in the elevator at Boston?"

"I vaguely remember a woman in the elevator on the trip to the academic conference, but to be honest, there have been so many 'trips in the elevator' where my attention was on more important things."

"Yes, that is most definitely true. Well anyway, she gave me her card, and we have kept in touch. She was quite impressed by your submission to me and she will be staying with us next week, while she's here on a business trip. You will get the spare room prepared when we arrive home."

I replied, "Yes, I'll be happy to."

I wondered what Athena had planned for me now.

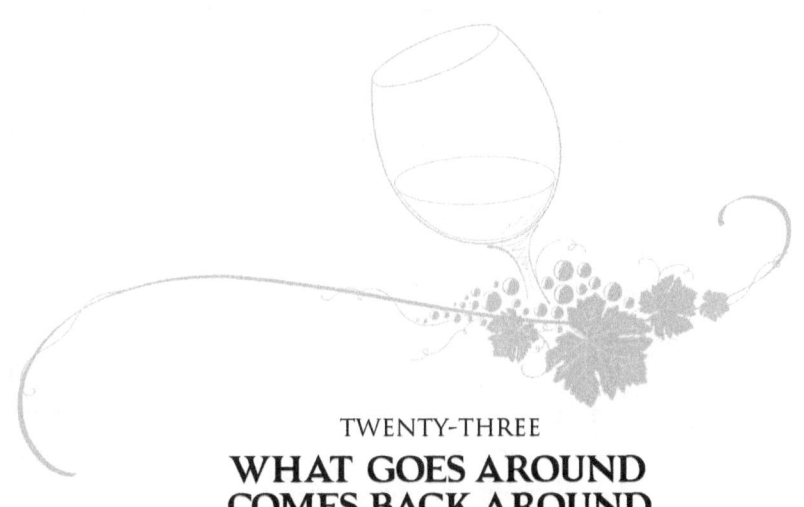

TWENTY-THREE

WHAT GOES AROUND
COMES BACK AROUND

"Whoa!" I heard Athena say in a startled tone of voice from the upstairs bedroom. I was on the main floor, doing laundry and dishes. I replied, "What is it? Is something wrong?" The tone of her voice told me she was surprised and somewhat apprehensive. She said nothing for a few minutes and finally said, "Could you come up here for a moment?" It may sound like a request to someone who doesn't understand our relationship. It was not. I stopped doing the chores I was doing and went upstairs. Athena was sitting in her office, staring at her computer with a look I had not seen in some time. It was a look that only came across her face when she talked about her childhood. A look that told me volumes about the way she was feeling. Quietly, I walked up behind her and placed my hand on her shoulder, slowly, firmly letting her know I was there and trying not to startle her. She reached back with her own hand and held mine. I asked, "What is it?" She was staring at a message she had received in an e-mail. Recently, she had put up a profile on a professional social network website used to connect professional people with similar skills. She was silent for a few moments and finally started to talk. "Did I ever tell you about my first duty station in the military?" "Yes," I replied, "it was at Vandenberg AFB in California." She had excelled immediately in the military, winning several awards as a new lieutenant. Nothing she had told me would have caused the reaction I was seeing now. She said, "Well, there was a guy there I had a huge crush on, it was a little bit embarrassing at the time, trying to manage being in a position of authority and then also being surrounded by people who were much more experienced and worldly. I was 24 years old then, a lot like I am now. Yet still, somehow kind of idealistic about some people." She continued, "This guy," as she pointed at the computer screen, "was there, and I was not shy about how interested I was in him. He was an intoxicating mix of sexuality and power. He had these piercing green eyes and was incredibly physically fit. I mean, like chiseled marble when he took his shirt off, only he was more like mocha marble. I never did know what his ethnicity was. He was not clearly any ethnicity. So I assumed he was multiracial. It was an intoxicating mix. I was really attracted to him." I nodded, listening. Athena had been with many men and women, both before we met and since I became her property. This is who she is, a powerful woman, with a very healthy sexual appetite. It was understood by both of us that this was the reality of our relationship early on. We spoke about it openly and honestly always. She sighed and continued. "I approached him, leaving no question I was interested in a sexual relationship with him. He was a Captain, and I was a Lieutenant, and I was working in the same building with him, watching him walk past my office daily was difficult. Everything about him was a sexual attraction to me. The way he looked at me, the way he smiled, the way he walked, and the way his uniform fit, it was nothing short of sexual perfection to me." I smiled. She was like this, so honest, so clear about how she felt at all times. It was an amazing thing to be the property of someone who could be so direct and so honest. I have never felt so comfortable with anyone at anytime. She continued, "Anyway, I approached him and suggested we meet for a drink, and maybe more? He smiled at me and said, 'I don't think so, little girl.' He humiliated me with that comment. He could have said, 'Thank you, but no,' or any other comment that was more respectful. I held him in such high regard, and maybe I should have done more homework on who he really was.

I was stunned as well. It was hard for me to imagine anyone being able to see Athena as anything but formidable, both intellectually and sexually. You would have to be blind not to be aware of who she was at the core. Apparently, this guy was either blind or stupid. Perhaps both, I thought, but I said nothing. Obviously, this was a memory that caused her discomfort. Something here was not yet settled, and she had no closure for this hurt she felt. She continued to stare at the e-mail. "So today I signed on to my e-mail, and guess who has sent me a message." I asked, "What's his name?" "He always went by his rank and last name when he was in my proximity, but I understood he liked to be called 'D', just 'D'. I never found out what it stood for. He was very mysterious. I was required to call him Captain Delcroix, like everyone else he outranked." I asked, "Does the e-mail address have his name somewhere on it?" She said it did not. She had looked, and there was his name. He had made some rank since they last met, and now his signature block included the title Colonel D. Delcroix, along with his current position at the Pentagon.

"May I read the e-mail?" I asked. She replied, "I will read it to you, sit down and tell me what you think." The e-mail was short and sweet. He said, "From your profile online, I see you have done well. Looks like you are with someone, but it is unclear if you are in a committed relationship from your profile. I will be in Colorado next month if you would like to go out for drinks." She stopped reading and said, "That's it, that's all he said. What are your thoughts, Edge?"

I thought about it a while before I replied, "I think he wants to get a drink. Let's go get a drink. Invite him here, and see what you think." She said, "You aren't a little bit concerned after all I have told you about him?" I said, "No. No matter what, I am your property; you know that, and I know that. What happens between you and anyone else will never change that fact, ever." We both already knew that in a way that words will never quite be able to describe. She smiled. All she said was, "Yes, true." Athena turned to the computer and started typing. She said, "How about some lunch, Edge?" Now she was dismissing me on one hand and reminding me that I would always be her property on the other. Much of what she said was like this, a consistent communication on multiple levels with every comment and look. Sometimes we communicated entire thoughts back and forth with just a look, intense eye contact, followed by under-standing and unquestionably knowing what the other felt and thought, with not a single word spoken.

Athena made contact with D, and for the next few weeks they texted, e-mailed and talked on the phone. They caught up on the events of their lives, each conversation becoming less and less formal, and more flirty and suggestive. Finally, D asked what was the relationship between me and Athena.

She explained simply my position as her property and that I would in no way inhibit or interfere with their revived relationship. He was silent on that for several minutes and then made the comment, "I see." Finally, they agreed on a plan for a weekend that D would be coming to Colorado to visit. Once Athena was off the phone, she asked me to find her a dress to wear to the airport to pick up D. She told me I would be driving her there, and the two of them back to our home. I asked, "What kind of dress would you like me to locate for you?" She thought for a minute and replied, "Surprise me, Edge! Something that would make you so hard, you would feel like you were 16 years old again. Hold nothing back, Edge. I mean to send a message during our meeting of my friend 'D'."

I started on the task of looking for a dress that would do just that. It took some time to locate the dress that I had in mind. Finally, I located it and asked her if she would like to see it before I ordered it. "Yes," she replied and casually walked to where I was seated at the bistro set in the nook of our large living room window. We ate dinner there often and watched the wildlife on the mountain from our window. The dress was a shimmery metallic fabric, which dropped tastefully to the knees. The shoulders were not bare, and there was a short loose and comfortable sleeve off each shoulder. It was not low cut, but there was a comfortably reserved neckline which would just barely hint at her ample breasts barely contained below. She smiled and said, "You are devious, this is excellent! Nothing about this is overtly sexual, except for one small detail." I smiled and said, "I hoped you would like it!" It was sheer, the metallic fabric was see-through and left nothing to the imagination. The cut of the dress was reserved, the fabric was not. It was exquisite and would fit her curvy body perfectly, but more important it would fit her mentally. There was no doubt this dress would set the tone for the weekend. The formal social formalities would be observed during our time with D; the underlying reality was, however, all bets were off and anything was possible.

TWENTY-FOUR

"D" DAY

Finally, the day arrived for us to drive to the airport and pick up D. Athena had made it clear she expected the car to be immaculate and that "D" was a stickler for cleanliness and attention to detail. She said, "I want you to make everything perfect for this weekend, Edge. If you wonder if some small detail needs to be done, do it." So that is exactly what I did. For several days before "D" arrived, I cleaned, polished, vacuumed and waxed. The linens were ironed and the floors shined. The windows were so clear, you would swear no glass was present. The house was perfect, every detail was taken care of. I would play my part perfectly. I would do whatever it took to make this weekend something that would heal the embarrassment Athena felt from so long ago. The car was ready, and I pulled it to the front of the house to pick up Athena at the front porch. Walking to the front door, I wondered what this weekend would bring. I had seen Athena determined before; however, this was a whole new level of mental preparation. Once inside our home, I called out, "The car is ready when you are." She responded, "Thank you, I will be right there." Moments later, she walked into the living room. The dress was beautiful by itself; however, now showing off her every line and curve, the dress was barely noticeable. I swallowed nervously. This was exactly how I saw her every day, physical beauty that was nearly lethal, and once you spoke to

her you had no doubt, intellectually, she definitely was lethal. The com-
bination was exactly what I had searched for in a woman my entire life. I
was reminded again how fortunate I was she owned me.

We arrived at the airport an hour or so later, parked the car, and
then walked to the waiting area. We were greeted with barely concealed
stares from men and women waiting for planes to land and passengers to
disembark. Athena was used to the attention and thought nothing of it.
It was just part of who she was; regardless of dress, people always stared
everywhere we went. Whether we were at a fast food restaurant or in a
nightclub, who Athena was caught people's attention immediately.

Finally, people started to file through the narrow walkway, and the
normal exclamations of happiness and excitement began. Long lost rela-
tives were reunited and families once again whole. Finally, here came "D".
Before Athena said, "There he is," I had already picked him out from the
crowd. The swagger was unmistakable. This was a man used to getting
everything he wanted, used to being looked at by women and having his
pick of eager sexual partners. I smiled. Athena said, "There he is in the
tight grey shirt." "Yes, I know," I replied. Athena's description of "D" was
near perfect. Striking green eyes and a physique that must have taken at
least 2 hours a day in the weight room to maintain. She was spot on in
her 14-year-old description of him. He walked up to her, obviously taking
in every curve and detail of her nearly nude body, with the exception of
the paper-thin metallic fabric clinging to her now admittedly trembling
body. Athena's hand was visibly shaking, and her nervous smile gave away
the carnal need she felt looking at this man. This was an ache she felt deep
inside, a wound that needed to heal. Athena embraced "D", and she kissed
him first softly, then deeply and passionately, moaning as his hands slid
down her back and then rested on her ass. Finally, she pulled away and
said, "Hey stranger, long time, no see!" He laughed comfortably. "Yes, it
has been a long time, and look how you have changed. It is Doctor now,
isn't it?" She smiled and said, "Yes, oh and let me introduce you to my
husband, and my property, this is Edge." D and I exchanged looks as he
attempted to size me up. "Property, huh? OK, whatever," and he stuck out
his hand. We shook hands, and I said, "Welcome, is it D, or does D stand
for something else, like Dementia?" He frowned. "D stands for Darius.
But only my closest friends call me Darius. You can call me 'D'." It had
worked, the battle lines had been drawn. "D" would be doing whatever he

could to get over on me from now on. That was the plan. I replied, "Cool with me, 'D'. Can I take your carry on while you and Athena get reacquainted?" He shrugged. "Sure, man, knock yourself out." I took the medium sized bag while he and Athena strolled ahead of me to the escalator and then down to the area luggage carousel, where his oversized luggage was just being loaded. "D" had already become comfortable with the idea I would get his luggage and pointed it out to me. His ego was being fueled as he stood arm in arm with my nearly nude Domme. People looked at them with appreciative stares, and I heard several men comment under their breath, "Lucky bastard". I smiled. Yes, he did appear to be very lucky. I walked up to the smiling couple and said, "All ready? I think I have it all now." Athena said, "Yes, let's go, and thank you, Edge." "D" said nothing to me and instead talked only to Athena, running his hand up and down the curve of the small of her back, occasionally dropping it to cup the curve of her ass as they walked ahead of me. I guess I was supposed to be jealous, maybe a normal man would be, but I am not normal. This is what I lived for, being owned by a powerful woman unafraid to be honest with me in any circumstance.

We walked to the car, and I loaded the luggage. "D" sat in the back seat, and I walked to the front passenger door to let Athena in. She said, "I'll be sitting in the back on the way home with my guest, Edge. Thank you." I smiled and opened the back door, and she climbed into the car. I drove us home while they talked and whispered in the back seat. Girlish giggles would erupt every now and then, and "D"'s deep baritone laugh also occasionally would roll like a subdued thunder through the car. I watched the road while they got reacquainted, that is, until I heard Athena sigh slightly. I took a quick look in the mirror and saw that "D" was holding her hand and then tried to slide his hand up her barely obscured thighs. The barely hidden caresses continued while I drove. Athena spoke like nothing was unusual, so as not to give away their intimate touching. Her timing was perfect; as we drove into the driveway of our home, she had just reached over and absentmindedly touched his swollen cock, still confined to his slacks, and said, "Oh look, we are nearly home. I am sorry, Edge, that was a quick trip." I smiled and said, "Yes, it was." She replied, "Will you get Darius' luggage from the back of the car and take it to his room while I show him the house?" "I would be happy to," I replied. D walked uncomfortably to the house while I removed the luggage. I did not envy him. Athena expertly manipulated his every move.

After showing "D" the house, she asked me to get out a bottle of wine and pour them each a glass. I poured while they sat and talked about old times and people they knew back at Vandenberg. She expertly turned the conversation back to him and what he had been doing with his life since they last met. "D" was happy to talk about himself, although I could see he barely concealed he was aching for a chance to continue what they had started in the back seat of the car. Athena toyed with him expertly, swirling her wine glass and making suggestive eye contact. She made seduction an art form.

I poured more wine as the night continued, and I saw her pick up her phone and begin texting. When she finished, she looked directly at me and then back to D. I understood immediately, she was ready to set her seductive plan in motion. I reached for my phone and read the instructions. I was to get up after pouring one more glass of wine and then state I had to do some computer work in the office. I would leave the room and not return until she texted me. She would record what happened with her carefully positioned iPad. I texted back, "OMW", our code that I was doing as she asked, I was "on my way".

I listened from upstairs as Athena moved to sit near "D" and then began her seduction. She had planned on getting him so drunk, he was unable to perform sexually. That was when she made her move and started to unzip his pants. She said, "My husband will be upstairs for some time. I think I need to taste you finally after all these years, don't you think?" Slurring his words, "D" said, "Shit, are you serious? I mean, he is just upstairs." She said, "I know," in a whisper, "let's be bad!" She pulled of his pants completely and started to caress his swollen and now throbbing cock. Later, I would watch as she expertly took him in her mouth and worked him ever closer to cumming, stopping every now and then to make a Shhhhh noise and hold a playful finger to her lips and point upstairs where I was sitting, listening to every sound at the top of the stairs. "We don't want my husband to be suspicious, now do we?" "D" whispered, "No, no, not at all, please keep going." Athena tormented him perfectly, bringing him to near climax several times, and then finally she said, "Well, maybe you have had too much wine, I can't seem to make you cum. I am sorry, 'D'." Moments later, my phone buzzed, and the text came through to come down and make dinner. So down the stairs I came, loud and quick. "D" struggled to get his pants back on and pretend nothing was going on. I said, "Sorry, I have been busy, hope things are still going all right. Would you both like dinner now?" "Yes," Athena said, "please start dinner while Darius and I catch up." She came to me and gave me a deep kiss; his scent still lingered on her swollen lips. D's glassy and barely focusing eyes widened as he watched her smile and continue on like nothing had happened. I made dinner as he started to sober up. I could not imagine the frustration he must have felt. So close to cumming from a secret blowjob from my slutty Domme wife, and yet not quite able to complete the deal.

TWENTY-FIVE

THE SEDUCTION

Dinner went off without a hitch, their conversation continued, and finally it was bed time. Athena dismissed "D" easily, saying, "Well, it has been a long day. I am beat. I guess we will see you in the morning, Darius," and kissed him on the cheek goodnight. The dejected look on his face was priceless. He turned and stumbled off to bed. We went to bed, undressing in the dark and whispering about the night's events. Her plan was working perfectly. She pressed her body against mine and said, "Phase 2 in a couple of hours." I did not know the plan; that, too, was part of the ownership. I had to watch it unfold and trust her. The anticipation was intense. I must have fallen asleep finally, because I was woken up by her whispering in my ear. "Edge, are you awake?" "Yes," I replied. "I am going down the hall, I will be back in a few hours. I want you to listen to everything and tell me how it feels to hear us fucking in the other room. I am going to give him a night he will never forget, and when I am done, I will be back to hear your thoughts. Tell me everything, every emotion, every thought." I agreed, and she got out of bed and walked down the hall to the guest bedroom. I heard her say, "Are you awake, 'D'?" He woke up and said, "Yes, what's wrong?" "Nothing," she replied, "my husband is asleep, he is a very deep sleeper, so I thought maybe we could fuck while he slept." He eagerly agreed. He tried to keep her quiet, but she claimed

I was an incredibly deep sleeper and nothing would wake me up. They fucked enthusiastically and loudly for some time. It was very intense to listen to a few feet away, lying in our bed, while she climaxed again and again. Finally, he was spent and fell asleep, and she got up and went to the bathroom. Then she returned to our bed. We whispered and laughed while we shared our version of the evening with the other. Her anxiety was gone, her mood much improved, and she curled up beside me and said, "OK, tell me how it felt to listen to us fuck." I admit, it was incredible, and I told her so. She also admitted Darius was exceptional in bed. He was everything she had dreamed of 14 years ago, and she said she had never had such intense orgasms, with anyone, ever. It was an admission I was grateful to hear. Her painful memory was gone, those demons exorcised with this intense sexual tryst.

In the morning, I got up and made breakfast. Athena did her usual routine or waking, checking e-mails in the office and then going downstairs to the gym in our basement to work out. She then showered and checked in on "D". She woke him up and asked him what he would like for breakfast. He asked for black coffee and eggs, with ham. "Great," she replied, "I will have Edge get started on it." I heard him reply, "Really? He is making us breakfast? I cannot believe he did not wake up last night." Athena replied, "Shhhh, our secret. He is a very deep sleeper; nothing wakes him up once he falls asleep." "D" replied, "No shit, because we were really loud, and damn girl, where did you learn some of that?" Again, I heard, "Shhh, he will hear you!!"

The day progressed as breakfast turned to lunch, and lunch to dinner as they barely kept hidden their sexual comments to each other while I pretended not to notice. This kind of honesty is intoxicating for me to be clear, and Athena knows it. For us, this is a gift to each other. To know without a doubt the other will not lie, no matter what. The nighttime arrived, and we went to bed. This night, Athena got up earlier and kissed me before softly walking down the hall and slipping into Darius' bed. The previous night was nothing compared to this episode of flesh pounding. The sound of skin slapping, carnal grunting, and even the air smelled of sex by the time they were finished. I heard them both gasping for air as they stopped to rest before going back at it. Sucking and moaning sounds came rolling down the hallway, and finally they were both exhausted. I fell asleep and woke up to Athena climbing back into bed.

She was covered in sweat and cum. She whispered, "Oh my God, Edge, that was unbelievable. I am so sore and swollen." I laughed and said, "I can imagine. It sounded amazing." She said, "Oh, it most definitely was, but now it is your turn, my cunt licking bitch." She climbed on top of me and gently lowered her sweaty and sticky ass onto my face. She whispered, "Be gentle, I am so sore, he really fucked me hard tonight." I gently did as she asked, and when she was finished with me, she rolled off and we both fell asleep.

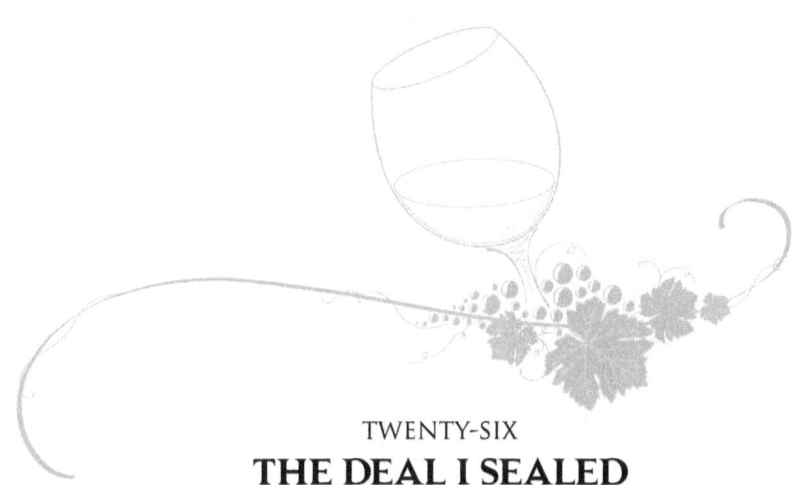

TWENTY-SIX

THE DEAL I SEALED

The next day, we took "D" back to the airport. He was totally convinced of his own superiority now and arrogantly made comments to her about how she should come with him to Washington, D.C. He had taken the bait, hook, line, and sinker. Athena owned his arrogant ass, and he did not even realize he had been used and was now about to regret the day he was so rude to her. I silently drove while she detailed the times she had tried to speak with him so long ago. How he had made her feel, and that the pain of that humiliation had haunted her for some time. She said, "I had hoped to show you this weekend the mistake you made back then." He tried to salvage the situation and agreed, but he stated he would make it up to her now. He had been wrong, that was obvious. He admitted it, but really, didn't she think their life together would be so much better than living with me? Athena smiled. "I am sure you are right, Darius, we obviously could have amazing sex. I mean, you fucked me like no one ever has, and I really like what you do for me. Isn't that what I told you, Edge?" "Yes! Yes, you did mention he was exceptional." Silence came from the back seat. "D" had nothing to say as we entered the parking lot and pulled into short-term parking. Athena continued, "Really, 'D', the only way this can continue is on a 'friends with benefits term'. If you would like to, perhaps we can meet up every so often here and in Washington,

D.C. I would like that very much; sexually, we are very compatible. But you have to understand this, nothing and no one will ever come between me and my Bitch, isn't that right, Edge?" I quietly nodded my head. "D" sat in the back seat, quietly looking out the window as we sat motionless in the parking stall. Several minutes passed, and finally he said, "OK, I guess I can live with that. I can be your 'friend with benefits', I mean, if that would be OK with you." Athena smiled and said, "Of course it is, Darius! That was how it was always meant to be; it just took you fourteen years to understand it." We all got out of the vehicle, I removed "D"'s luggage, and we walked him to the ticket counter. As we approached security, "D" turned to me and said, "You were awake and listening the whole time, weren't you?" I said, "Yes, I was." He said, "And you went upstairs knowing what she had planned that first day, am I right?" I replied, "I did have some idea of what she planned." He looked around the airport and rubbed his head, confused, amazed and said, "Oh man, you really are her property!" I said, "Yes, I am." "OK, man, OK…well, Edge, till we meet again," and extended his hand. I shook the hand of the man my wife had ravaged shamelessly for the past two days and smiled. "Welcome to our world, 'D'." Athena gave him a hug and a deep kiss and said, "I really hope we can do this again soon," while she casually fondled his cock through his pants in front of security officers who watched us. I heard one of them say to the other, "Whoa, there is a lucky guy!" Smiling at them, Athena turned back to "D" and said, "I really do!"

THE
WINE
CLUB II

SPECIAL PREVIEW
RELEASING 2016

ONE

THE WHITE RABBIT

I n California, there are several regions famous for wine, and we are going to visit them all!"

I smile and nod as I watch the road, listening to the trip that Athena has mapped out for us. We are on our way to one of the many first-rate wine growing regions that California is famous for. I drive while she explains the itinerary and then names the different vineyards and wineries we will visit on this trip. She reads to me from her iPad the history of each of the regions and vineyards. She explains there are six regions in California famous for growing wine, and each region has its own specialty. As she delves deeper into wine lore, I notice a sign that announces a rest stop 8 miles ahead. The more she explains, the deeper into the trance I go. I am not sure what it is…perhaps it is about her intellect, or the ways she describes the regions? Maybe it is her voice, smooth like satin and calming. Regardless, I know we will be stopping at the rest area; populated or not, it doesn't matter. Actually, it does matter, I want the world to see how I adore her and worship her. Years ago I was ashamed of this need, now I embrace it, it is no longer a battle to just exist with no chance of fulfillment. I secretly hope there is a crowd that will gather and watch as she again lets me assume the role of her property, subordinate to her alone, willing to do whatever she desires. I have to pull over at the rest stop because I can no longer focus, simply driving a car is difficult. The need to be the sexual property of this amazing woman is overwhelming, and I can barely breathe. I feel drugged as I struggle to bring the vehicle to a safe stop. Athena looks up from her iPad and then turns to me, a questioning look in her eye. She sees the undeniable longing, the need to feel once again that I am unquestionably her property. Smiling, she says, "Ahh, I see that you are planning a public display of our relationship. Come with me, my faithful bitch, it is time you worshipped me. It has been too long, hasn't it?" I can barely say the words, "Yes, far too long."

We walk among the desert fauna as she names off the different plants the Department of Transportation has planted to decorate the rest stop. Choosing low maintenance plants capable of surviving with little care and water. We are in the middle of the desert, it is nearly noon and very few people are at the rest stop. Surprisingly, there are no bugs and the breeze is comfortable. Athena strolls ahead of me and lightly brushes the hem of her white cotton sun dress with one hand while she randomly turns this way and that, searching for the place that fits her mood. I never know what she will choose on these outings. Sometimes she is blatantly sexual and voyeuristic. For example, in the Atlanta Airport last month, while riding the airport tram from one terminal to the other, she backed me into a corner, forced me to my knees and covered my head with her dress while I buried my face between her legs. I was on my knees for a very long time as she rode me rhythmically, gasping each time she climaxed, and when she finally let me up, I was covered in her cum and surrounded by people, all staring at me silently. Some approving, some very disturbed and alarmed. Athena did not care, she smiled a warm, disarming smile at all of them and said firmly, "There is nothing like owning a man that knows his proper place in life." Several people smiled, some laughed, others pretended not to know what had been going on. I know personally every time she put me on display like this, it filled a dark need I have never been able to explain. I really craved to be undoubtedly owned, to have no question of my place in her life. It was a feeling of safety I have never been able to successfully explain.

Athena has picked a table that faces the nearby freeway and tells me to crawl under the table. I do as she tells me, and soon I am where I so desperately need to be while she continues to read to me about the different wine regions of California. I take that as a challenge and do my best to make her lose her train of thought. She continues to read out loud, and then I hear the footsteps of three or four people walking across the pea-sized gravel to a nearby table. There is a partition between their picnic table and ours. I listen as they set the table, preparing for their lunch. Athena pulls my head from between her legs and motions for me to be silent, gently placing her finger across my wet, cum-stained lips. She motions for me to come out from under the table, and as I do she sits on the edge of the table, pulling her dress up and smiling, she smiles playfully as she quietly unzips my pants. She pulls my cock out and jumps off the table. Changing her mind, she whispers in my ear, "Now it is your turn to be quiet, you tortured me, let's see how well you do," as she drops to her knees and expertly works the tip of my cock with her lips and tongue. I gasp loudly as she gently bites me, knowing my appetite for pain and sex is matched only by her need to provide it. Smiling, she laughs a small, playful laugh. I am a toy to be used for her pleasure only, we both know that, and it is just the way it should be.

The picnic-eating group is just a few feet away, separated by only a windbreak. Athena works me into a sweat-soaked frenzy in no time and then stops just as I am gritting my teeth, about to cum. She smiles as she stops and shakes her head silently no, no, no, as she stops tormenting me. She breathes heavily as she turns away from me and hikes her dress up over her hips, spreading her legs, she lies across the table and whispers just loud enough for me to hear, "I want you to fuck me as hard as you can. Pull my hair, pound me. Do it now! I want to feel your desperate need to be mine!" A few minutes of hips slapping together, scratching, biting and hair pulling, we both cum, covered in noonday desert sex sweat. Gasping for air, we giggle like adolescents, whispering and pulling our clothes back on. Athena turned and kissed me and said, "You smell like my pussy, I like that! I have marked you. For the rest of the day, I want to smell my cum on you whenever I kiss you. Do you understand?" I do. I need this, and she somehow knows this instinctively.

We walked from behind the partition separating our table from the lunch eating group, and as we walk past them we are greeted with knowing stares and silence from the group. I guess we were not all that quiet. Athena smiles at them and says innocently, "Hello!" We are back on the road moments later, the rest stop behind us, and my mind is once again clear, safely assured of my place in Athena's world.

We attended many wineries in California, but one winery rose above them all as our favorite. It was a small winery that produced an amazing red Zinfandel. And it became our new favorite, complex, spicy and bold, the complexity of the flavors they had melded into one bottle was unprecedented. The Winery was Doce Robles. If you ever get a chance to attend a tasting there, we both highly recommend it.

Out trip to California was mainly about business, mixed with some pleasure. We finally ended up at Athena's friend Bliss' house. As we pull up to the house, I realize that it is only one block from the beach. Getting out of the car, I can hear the waves crashing against the shoreline and the distinct bark of California gray sea lions. The smell of the Pacific Ocean permeates the air. Athena explains that her friend is not at home and will not be until later today. She is at class still but left the front door open for us. I unload the car while Athena walks around her friend's home, admiring the many books that fill every shelf and flat space. Her friend is a self-proclaimed nerd and introvert, although I have yet to see the introvert in her. At least not as I understand the term. She is very outgoing, successful, and when she does speak out, her comments are well thought out and leave no doubt of a very nimble and capable mind. Her exceptional mind is masked by twinkling, playful blue eyes, framed with jet black curly hair. The affect of her gaze combined with the depth of understanding and the intellect implied in the comments she makes, make for any trip or time spent with the two of them together to be a challenge, at the very least. Regardless, for the time being Bliss is not home, and for now at least I have only one woman to attend to.

I unpack and put our clothing away and then begin looking for the washer and dryer; we have been on the road a week, and I need to wash the clothes. Searching the home, I cannot find any washer or dryer. Puzzled, I search again, room to room and closet to closet. Nothing. I am baffled. Finally, Athena smiles and says, "Edge, we are on the West Coast. The washer and dryer will be on the outside of the home. The temperature never drops low enough or long enough here to damage them, so everyone keeps them on the outside of the house." Eyebrows raised, I go outside the home, and sure enough the washer and dryer are on the outside of the home, on the patio and full of laundry. Now what do I do? I don't feel comfortable rifling through Bliss's laundry or doing it for her. I decide our laundry can wait, and I explain to Athena that I can't do laundry, and why.

Athena laughs and says, "Poor Bliss. She is so busy with school and career, she must have forgot about her laundry. Who knows how long the clothes have been out there? I would be the same way if you did not take care of everything for me. You do realize that, don't you?" I smile. It feels good to know it makes her as happy for me to serve her as it makes me. I remember briefly what I felt like before Athena, it was not pretty. Smoldering on a low, a much less painful flame of rage is still there, not quite extinguished, but definitely held at bay by Athena's steady and strong hand. I wish I could end the rage that occasionally flares up, reminding us both of who I was before Athena broke me and then trained me, making me realize what it was I had been looking for, for so damn long. I was hers now, and owned; that was what I needed, and now I understood that. This is what I was born to be.

A few hours later, the garage door opens and a sleek black SUV backs into the driveway. I try not to let on that the internal battle is about to begin. I head to the back of the house to try to delay the meeting that it is about to happen. Ridiculous, I know, but it is hard to hide the anxiety being in the room with the two dominant women causes me. What used to be expressed as rage and anger is now admiration. I have a lifetime of experience with rage and how to express it, not so much experience with admiration, and an undeniable instinctive need to serve them both. It is awkward, to say the least.

I stare out the window at the back of the house at the still unwashed laundry sitting in the unused washer and dryer, thinking....it is not so easy to not immediately want to take care of them both, in every way possible, but it is not a thought I can let see the light of day. I have mentioned it several times to Athena, and she agrees it would be ideal for all of us, but she explained, "Bliss is not there yet, she does not know who she is yet and what she really needs, let's give her time." I have thought about this comment often. How do you really know what you need unless you are painfully honest with yourself? Anyway, in my mind I am preparing for the image of Bliss standing in her living room. Greeting us both, wearing her military uniform, rank insignia, branch of service all visible. The neutral image is reassuring, I am pretty sure that this will be the image I will see when I return to the living room after the brief moment spent breathing deeply in the back bedroom. I walk back to the front of the house, pretending to be calm and relaxed, and I am floored by the image I see. Bliss is wearing a short denim skirt and tight fitting cotton shirt. She smiles the bright smile that I remember from the last trip she made to our home in Colorado and walks forward to give me a brief hug and welcome. I say hello, but in the back of my head I am thinking, "Thank God I am not in any classroom with this woman wearing this outfit, I would be a basket case." I remember the frustration I felt when I first met Athena at being so close, but so far away from her. That same feeling is back. I turn away from Bliss as she walks into her bedroom and closes the door, changing into something "more relaxed". Athena smiles a knowing smile at me, her eyes twinkling as she remarks, "Not what you had imagined in your head, was it?" I play dumb, hoping that I'm not that see-through, and reply, "What do you mean?" She giggles. "What she would wear to school. I saw your face and the way you struggled to keep yourself in check." I sigh deeply. "Yes, not what I expected at all."

Later that night, after I have made them both dinner and cleaned up the dishes, I mentioned to Bliss that I would like to do some laundry. She said, "Sure, go ahead, the machines are on the patio." I told her that I had found them already but that there were clothes in each. She was surprised. "Really? There are? I wonder how long those clothes have been out there! Oh wow, I totally forgot about them." Athena smiled as she watched our interaction, and later as we lay in bed she remarked, "She needs someone to be her property and keep her on track, take care of her every need, someone like you." I smile at that thought as I drift off to sleep. In my head, the incredible fantasy of what that would be like, being the property of the two amazing women, is light years away from what the reality would be. I would experience the reality of what that fantasy meant soon enough.

The rest of the week was spent hitting all of the local wineries, taste testing their best and finding most of it was lacking. Paso Robles turned out to be our favorite region, and nothing in Monterey compared. We visited Cannery Row and a few of the other notable sites, but to be honest, nothing compared with the early morning walk on the beach. Every morning, I would wake up and walk the block or so to the beach. Every morning, the beach was different; some days there were porous rocks that had washed up, other days huge sections of seaweed that had broken loose from the large kelp forests just offshore were deposited. Sea lions cruised the waves, patrolling back and forth, barking and then disappearing for several minutes, only to reappear a little further down the beach. This was my daily routine, the beach and then back to the house to make breakfast and coffee.

The night before we were planning to leave, Athena asked Bliss, "So where to after school? Do you know what your assignment will be?" Bliss thought for a moment and finally said, "I have several options in the works right now. I don't know for sure which will pan out, but most likely I will be in or near Washington, D.C., either at the Pentagon or the C.I.A. At least that is the plan."

I was quiet during the conversation; it was unimaginable to me to work at either place. Moments like this make me realize exactly how remarkable they both really are. While I am lost in my own thoughts, I am somehow aware that Athena is making a comment about how she, too, has several options "on the table" and is waiting to see which pans out. Panic strikes me instantly. Options? I know nothing stays the same, and especially as driven as they both are, to expect to remain in Colorado on our mountain for any extended period of time is unreasonable. But the comment has caught me off guard. I had no clue there were options "on the table." I say nothing and wait for Athena to elaborate. She doesn't; she just leaves the comment there, hanging in the air. Finally, we go to bed and I expect that she will explain the comment. She does not; she simply says goodnight and falls to sleep. I don't fall asleep for several hours; suddenly, everything doesn't feel so safe and permanent.

The next day, I pack the car and we leave early, headed back towards Colorado. I know that when she is ready Athena will explain the "options on the table" comment, and I actually convince myself that perhaps it is nothing to worry about. Perhaps it was just a comment meant to keep the conversation going, small talk, just chatter. Deep down, though, I know Athena doesn't know the meaning of mindless chatter, this is not some off-hand comment without a purpose. I will just have to be patient.

A month has passed since we left California, and there has been no mention of the "options on the table" comment. There is an unspoken tension in the air, as I wait for her to explain the comment. Athena knows I am waiting, curious about the meaning behind the comment, but she won't show her hand. So… I wait.

One day, I returned from buying groceries and came into the house carrying many of the plastic sacks so commonly used to carry groceries. I had way too many of them in each hand, and it took me several attempts to get the door open that allowed access from the open garage to the basement of our home. As I slowly climbed the stairway to the main floor, I heard Athena talking on her phone. I only heard brief pieces of the conversation, but it was clear a negotiation was underway. "I promise you that you will not regret this, and besides, you do owe me, remember? Yes, I know, but trust me, this will benefit you more than you can possibly understand. I had no idea this relationship could be so beneficial, and in so many ways I never imagined. Sooo, are we in agreement? Good. I will let him know tonight. See you soon." And then she hung up. I came through the doorway into the living room from the basement and unloaded the groceries onto the island in the middle of the kitchen. "How did it go?" she asked. I replied that it went well, the store was not busy and I was able to acquire all the food items that she preferred.

"Good, were you able to get the steaks I asked you to buy?"

"Yes."

"Excellent. We will have them tonight, we have much to discuss. Choose a Malbec that will compliment the meat, and I would like dinner at 6." It is not a demand, but a statement; by now, we each know our roles in this relationship.

The time has come, that is clear. Tonight, I will find out the meaning of the statement she made a month ago. The anticipation weighs heavily on my mind, and I completely forget about the conversation I overheard while coming up the stairs moments earlier. The day passes me by at a surprisingly rapid rate. Hitting the gym in the basement, cleaning the house, laundry, and then preparation for dinner. Finally, we are sitting in the living room and listening to Loreena Mckinnett. There are several candles lit, and as Loreena starts to sing the lyrics to "The Mummers Dance", Athena smiles, sighs and begins to talk. I listen.

I don't remember when the music stopped, but it did. The music was a distant memory. My wine glass was empty, but I don't remember drinking any of the smoky Malbec it contained. I was deep in thought, deep inside myself, quiet and taking inventory of the thoughts that juggled in my head. I don't know how long I was quiet or how long I sat there. Finally, I was startled by someone touching my hand.

"Are you all right?" Athena asked. I am not sure that I can honestly answer the question yes or no.

"I want to be sure that you heard exactly what I said, so please repeat back to me what you heard, I don't want there to be any misunderstanding," she says in a quiet but firm voice.

It takes me a minute to reply, but finally in a voice that feels very far away and cold I hear myself saying that she has been offered a job overseas, working for her company in a capacity that will be shoring up NATO in response to the Russian invasion of Ukraine. I will not be able to accompany her, and she has no idea how long she will be gone. The mission is Top Secret, and she has had to undergo an extensive background investigation. That was why she had not kept me informed of the possible change in our lives; she was not sure she would be offered the job.

"Yes," she replies, "that is correct. Do you remember anything else?"

"You have made plans for me to stay with Bliss, and that I will take care of her while you are gone."

"Yes, we have made the arrangements for you to belong to her while I am gone. Understand this, Edge, you are still mine, I am not leaving you. I am just going to be gone for a while. While I am gone, you will belong to Bliss, unquestionably and completely. Are we clear?"

"Yes, clear. Very clear."

"It will be a difficult adjustment, I am sure, but I am confident you will do fine. I have to leave in two days. You will stay behind and prepare the house and vehicles for our extended absence. When everything is done, you will fly to meet Bliss."

I ask, "Where was she assigned? I mean, after she graduates, what is her follow on assignment? Does she know yet?"

"No, not yet. She thinks that it has been narrowed down to either the CIA or a special duty assignment at the Pentagon. Regardless, you will do everything possible to help her make the transition. Understood?"

"Yes."

Two days later, I drive Athena to the airport and accompany her inside to check in her luggage. I have packed everything she told me she would need, and a few extras she may not expect. Our favorite music on CDs, and a flash drive with pictures of our home in Colorado, the deer, mountain lions, bear and eagles. Some things to remind her of our home. Her favorite sweatshirt, it belonged to me, but she has since adopted it as her own. I bought it on our trip to Boston, at Boston College. Good memories there, especially in the library, or "Hogwarts", as our guide explained the students refer to the library because of its appearance. Anyway, she is gone. A smile, a kiss, and a look that said volumes. She walked through the security lines and disappeared.

I am home now, I don't remember the drive back from the airport. The house is suddenly huge, quiet and feels ominous, and somehow already empty. It has only been a few hours since I put her luggage in the car and opened the door for her as she sat in the passenger seat, excited and nervous about her new opportunity. Home is not home without her. I feel anxiety, and I know I must keep moving if I am to survive. Movement is survival, I learned that early on in life. Keep moving; no matter what, keep moving.

I have not cranked up the stereo in some time. I have been at peace for years. Listening to Mozart, opera, soothing music. Now, however, I am rifling through old boxes, looking for the music I used to listen to before her, before I found peace. Before the storm in my soul was quieted by her strength and dominance. Soon, Ronnie James Dio is screaming out "Holy Diver", and Fight, led by vocalist Rob Halford, is grinding out the surly and dark lyrics to "Immortal Sin." Darkness is once again in my vision. Darkness and barely controllable rage. It is only day one.

In less than a week, I have the house ready, winterized, perishable food removed. The vehicles are stored in the garage on blocks, the gasoline in the tanks treated with fuel stabilizer, and batteries removed. I spend most of the day in the gym in the basement and sleep on the couch. The bed is too big, and I can't sleep more than a couple of hours at a time anyway. Finally, the phone rings, and it is Bliss. She is less than happy and explains that she did not get the assignment that she had hoped for. She will be working at the Pentagon. She will have no time to pick me up from the airport, as she works a very strenuous schedule. She rapidly spits out an address to have a cab take me to once I arrive at the airport and then asks if I have any questions. As I take in a breath to say, "No," she hangs up on me. I save her number to my phone and type in her name. This should be fun.

I call the airline and make the reservation to fly out the next day. The timing is no notice, and the flights are expensive, with long layovers in O'Hare. I will arrive at the Ronald Reagan International Airport in

Virginia at midnight. Fucking wonderful. Finding a cab at midnight should be a bitch, this after a day of flying, one of my least favorite things to do. At least I can look forward to staying with Bliss and the gift she and Athena have agreed to provide me. I am hopeful of the potential of the relationship. Bliss is someone that I do find intriguing, and one of only two women I have found that instinctively calm the emotional storm that rages inside of me. Like Athena, she doesn't know how to be anything but exceptional, and casual conversation with either of them can be intoxicating. I smile at the memories of the times she has spent in our home in Colorado and remember the unquestionable relief I felt at being so expertly owned. She had no problem accepting my status as property to be used; not loved, not coddled. Clearly, darkly and domi-nantly owned. Like a car that needs to be driven to stay in good running shape, Athena has handed her the keys to my dark and twisted soul and told her, "Drive this bitch like you own him." I am admittedly excited and apprehensive. Somehow, in the back of my mind there is a small, quiet voice saying, "Everything could never be this easy." My life has been a battle from day fucking one, and change always means chaos and pain. Always. Still, somehow I hold on to the idea in my head that all will be fine. Athena has made the arrangements, and Bliss is the only other woman I have known who makes me feel safe. Outside of this very small circle of capable and exceptional women, my life has been a brutal, fucked up war zone. Those painful memories echo loudly, and as the day goes on, the echo gets louder and more ominous.

TWO
ARRIVAL

Early the next morning, I get up, shower and call a cab. Twenty minutes later, the yellow Chevy Caprice pulls into the long gravel driveway and heads towards the house. I lock the front door and quickly step down onto the front steps of the huge porch at the front of our mountain home. The driver pops open the trunk from inside the car, never making a move to get out of the car and help me load my luggage into the trunk of the older yellow cab I have called to take me to the airport. It is still dark, and the driver (whose appearance is similar to a human version of Jabba the Hut from the Star Wars movies) looks like I have woken him up from what I assume is a nap, taken nightly I am sure, when most of his would be clients are sound asleep. Not today! I say hello to him and introduce myself. He rolls his eyes at my enthusiasm and energy and reaches up with one meaty hand, slamming shut the plexiglass window that separates the back seat from the front seat. Quietly, I look out the window and watch as what has been the safest place I have ever known disappears in the pre-dawn light. Moments later, I smile as I realize a few years ago before I met Athena, I would have responded angrily to such a display. I would have confronted the overweight and lazy cabbie and made damn sure that he never showed me such a lack of respect again. He would have remembered with real fear the "angry psycho nut case" he picked up in the mountains for years to come. I breathe deeply, sigh and watch as the scenery changes from remote mountain landscape to an urban and modern city. A long, very silent hour and a half later, we arrive at the airport. Once the driver is paid and my luggage has been retrieved from the truck, I set out and hit the ticket counter. My long day of traveling 500+ miles per hour, several miles above the Earth is about to begin.

Sitting in seat 16 B, I am trapped. Seat 16 A is taken by the single largest producer of natural gas in North America, disguised as a middle-aged grandmother who (unrequested by me) has begun to give me her entire life history. She is letting loose barely audible sulfuric bursts of intestinal gasses. In mid-sentence, mumbling, "God bless" quietly to herself, she continues talking about her amazing 6-year-old grandson, Johnny Ray. Seat 16 C is taken by what appears to be a 16-18-year-old "princess" who is giving me the most hateful and evil looks, each and every time a cloud of putrid smelling gas unmercifully floats past me to her throne near the aisle. The Princess has covered her mouth and nose with a recently (and repeatedly) perfumed scarf. I can barely make out her mumbling angrily something about a "sick motherfucker" as she glares at me with hateful dark eyes. This will be a horrendously long flight!

Finally we land at O'Hare, and I turn on my cell phone to check for messages from Bliss. There are none. The pilot thanks us for using their airline and welcomes us to Chicago. Current temperature and weather information is given out as we taxi to the terminal. "Lindsey Lohan" to my right is on her phone telling someone that the flight has been awful, all due to the "sick fuck" she has been sitting next to. Somewhere, there is a man (or woman) who is enjoying their life. I can see them walking down the street smiling, totally unaware that their life is going to be destroyed by this acidic little gem of humanity. I gave up trying to explain that the toxic shit floating in the air was not mine and embraced my inner child. Every time Grandma lets loose, blessing herself quietly, I would turn and gaze, smiling at the princess. Raising my eyebrows rapidly up and down with glee as another chemical attack was unleashed and wafted towards Her Majesty. I may not be the initiator of the chemical attack, but I can sure as hell be the antagonist if provoked.

I walk through the airport in no rush at all. The fight has me laying over for several hours, and I am stuck here. Watching the surges of people hurry past me in the terminal, I am struck by the thought somewhere

Athena is possibly walking past in another terminal, perhaps on the other side of the planet, maybe she is in Frankfurt, or Istanbul, who knows, she could be anywhere. In a ridiculous attempt to not become homicidally depressed, I pretend that if I watch carefully enough, I may see her walk past. So I scan the crowds, playing out the fantasy in my head that she is here and for a brief moment I will see her and we stop and eat lunch together, commenting on "what are the odds?". Soon enough, I lose interest in this mental masturbation and get up and just walk the terminals. Three hours later, I have travelled all of the sections of O'Hare that are available for passengers to walk. No telling how many miles I have walked, but I did find out there are terminals 1,2 and three, but the maps show no Terminal #4; curious, I thought. They have a terminal#5, but no #4. Anyway, I counted 123 food and beverage outlets and learned that the airport has over 25,000 parking places. Yes, this is a very long layover!

Finally, I text Bliss. I don't know what to say, so I say, "Hi! Landed in O'Hare, just checking in to let you know where I am and that I am looking forward to seeing you." I push send. The message is delivered; after 35 minutes of no response, I give up checking and put the phone away. Maybe she is busy? Yeah, she is probably very busy, I tell myself, no need to worry. In the back of my head, the ominous echo of past relationship nightmares are rolling forward again.

Finally, as I settle in to my new seat on the flight from O'Hare to Ronald Reagan airport, my phone vibrates; hopefully, Bliss has replied. The phone shows one message, and the source is unknown. Weird, I have never had a text show up with an unknown number. I open the text, and there is a picture of what is unquestionably the Eiffel Tower. No message; just a picture of the tower. What the hell is this? Could it be from Athena? I want it to be, so I save the picture. Not a single comment from Bliss.

Approaching the Ronald Reagan National Airport, I see that we are following the path of a river. The co-pilot comes over the intercom to explain that we are following the path of the Potomac River to the airport and that we will be arriving shortly. I looked out the window on my left and was surprised to see the Arlington National Cemetery and the Pentagon. Colorado feels far away as we slowly coast in and the plane announces with an abrupt shudder that the rear wheels have touched down.

The past two hours, I have been banging on the door of 833 19th Street in Crystal City, Virginia. This is the address that Bliss told me was her new residence. When I arrived, her black SUV was in the driveway. The cab that brought me here was driven by a dude named Emilio, and he was the only person I have met this entire trip that wasn't a royal pain in the ass. Emilio said the area Bliss lived in was heavily populated by Pentagon workers and the locals called it the "Bone Yard". I asked why, and he said that many military careers ended abruptly here. The Pentagon was considered a meat grinder of an assignment, and only the best and most ruthless survived the politics which dominate the building.

I replied, "Ya, I can imagine."

He said, "Really, you have no idea. I have taken so many people to the airport from the Bone Yard. They arrive happy and full of hope, they leave broken, shattered and bitter. I don't know what the hell goes on in that building, but it must be intense. So you be on the lookout, ya hear me?"

I nodded.

Emilio wished me luck in the "Bone Yard", and after I tipped him heavily, we fist bumped. He started to drive away and then stopped. He got out of the cab and walked back to me and handed me a card with his cell number on it.

He said, "Hey, Edge, you ever need a ride, you call me, and I will come pick you up. Be cool!"

I said thanks and headed to the front door of what was to be my home for who knows how long.

Still no answer. Frustrated, I decided to go out and walk the area and get a feel for the neighborhood. Crystal City was anything but "crystal." It was an older area, single story wood frame houses were mixed with two story brick homes. Nothing about the area suggested affluence or gave any hint to the powerful positions the people living here held. To be honest, it looked run down, and much like the inner city I used to work in so many years ago. I did notice no gunshots ringing out in the night, and the cars were mostly new. A half hour later, I came back to the door and tried one last time to get an answer. Knocking hard, I struck the door three times. As I was about to strike a fourth time, the deadbolt was thrown back, I heard a chain lock being removed, and the door opened. I was relieved at first, and then speechless.

Bliss stood at the door, totally nude, sleepy-eyed, disheveled black hair hanging in her face, and more than a little bit irritated. She motioned impatiently for me to come in and turned, walking back into her new home.

The picture is still burned in my mind as I admittedly admired her ass as she walked away. She pointed at the couch and said, "Sleep there, and try to be quiet. I have to get up early tomorrow." Just like that, she turned and walked away from me and walked down the short hallway to her bedroom. No apology for leaving me locked out for the past two plus hours. No "Hi", "Welcome", or even a "Drop to your knees, bitch" (I could hope). No, this was my welcome to Virginia, barely acknowledged and shunned to the couch. My new role as Bliss' property has started.

ABOUT THE AUTHOR

Edge Steele resides in the United States with his Domme. When not serving the needs of his amazing mistress, he enjoys photography and finding epicurean delights to please the center of his universe. He loves to learn. Science fiction, opera, food, and wine are just a few of his passions. He now realizes life is too short to waste living in denial of who we are and hopes you will enjoy these stories.